Running down the hill 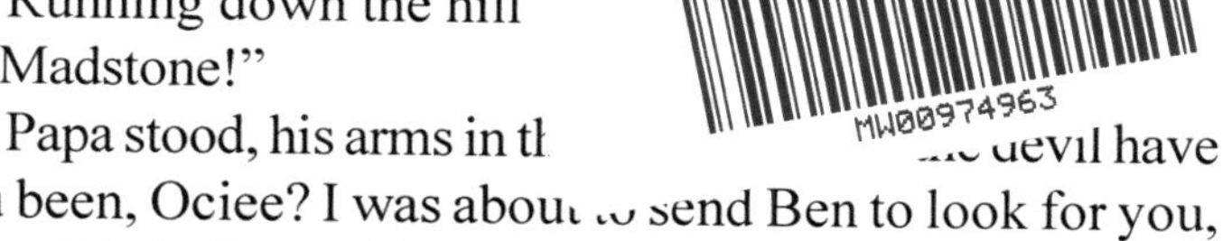
the Madstone!"

Papa stood, his arms in tl ... ...devil have you been, Ociee? I was abou... ...send Ben to look for you, Ociee Nash. Dag nabit!"

Papa had never been as angry with me, not in my whole life.

Miz Annie Kate, holding her long black skirt, waved her hand and pointed to the bag with the Madstone. She dropped down beside my brother Fred, opened her pouch and dropped the Madstone in the milk. Then she applied it to Fred's arm, securing it with a white rag.

In fear and disbelief, Fred stared at the rock, which, by then, was stuck firmly to his arm. "The dern thing is sucking on my arm!"

Amazingly, the swelling from the snake bite started going down.

"Thank glory," I said.

"As long as we're being thankful, Ociee Nash," said Miz Annie Kate, "let's be thankful for *you* going for help."

I did ride mighty fast and without falling off. Papa put his hands on my shoulders. "Ociee Nash, it's plain to see you're smart, and brave, and a fine horsewoman. I should not have gotten so angry. Please, will you forgive me?"

"Yes, Papa." I hugged tight to him.

I didn't want to let on too much, but I *was* mighty pleased with me.

About the Ociee Nash series

A few years ago, Georgia author Milam McGraw Propst wrote A FLOWER BLOOMS ON CHARLOTTE STREET, a turn-of-the-century story based on the real girlhood adventures of her grandmother, Ociee Nash. That book won Milam honors as Georgia Author of the Year and received a national Parent's Choice Fiction recommendation.

A movie producer liked the book and turned it into the film THE ADVENTURES OF OCIEE NASH, which introduces Skyler Day as Ociee, Keith Carradine as Ociee's dad, Mare Winningham as her colorful Aunt Mamie, and a young actor named Ty Pennington (now the star of EXTREME MAKEOVERS) as one of the famous Wright brothers who Ociee meets while visiting North Carolina.

Next Milam wrote a second book about her grandmother's childhood, OCIEE ON HER OWN. Now Milam is pleased to continue the story in THE FURTHER ADVENTURES OF OCIEE NASH. You can visit Milam's website at www.milammcgrawpropst.com, and learn more about the film of her first book at www.ociee.com.

For information on Milam's novel for adults, CREOLA'S MOONBEAM, visit www.bellebooks.com

The Further Adventures of Ociee Nash

Milam McGraw Propst

Dear Helen – this might be my grandmother's favorite story!

Milam

Smyrna, Georgia

This is a work of fiction. Names, characters, places and incidents are either the products of the author's imagination or are used fictitiously. Any resemblance to actual persons (living or dead,) events or locations is entirely coincidental.

Bell Bridge Books
PO BOX 67
Smyrna, GA 30081

ISBN: 978-0-9841258-0-7

Bell Bridge Books is an Imprint of BelleBooks, Inc.

Copyright 2009 by Milam McGraw Propst

Printed and bound in the United States of America.

All rights reserved. No part of this book may be reproduced in any form or by any electronic or mechanical means, including information storage and retrieval systems, without permission in writing from the publisher, except by a reviewer, who may quote brief passages in a review.

We at BelleBooks enjoy hearing from readers. You can contact us at the address above or at BelleBooks@BelleBooks.com

Visit our websites – www.BelleBooks.com
and www.BellBridgeBooks.com.

10 9 8 7 6 5 4 3 2 1

Cover Design: Debra Dixon
Cover photo credits:
Girl photo - C Pavel Vlasov - Fotolia.com
Boxes - C Inna Felker - Fotolia.com
Texture - C Jill Battaglia - Dreamstime.com
Interior design: Linda Kichline

Chapter 1

The year 1900
Abbeville, Mississippi

"Jump, Ociee! JUMP!"

Jump? I couldn't budge. Bare feet frozen to the flatcar floor, my legs were as unbending as the trunk of our dead pecan tree. My heart pounded in perfect rhythm with the locomotive's thunderous rumble. With every breath, we roared faster and faster down the railroad tracks.

The empty flatcar should have been carrying pine logs, not me, an eleven year old Mississippi girl.

"Help me, Mama!" I clutched her locket.

The flatcar hadn't seemed high seconds ago when my brother Ben boosted me on it. But how could I be scared? I was Ociee Nash. I'd been swinging on ropes from our hayloft since I was four years old.

Our barn never moved fast as the wind.

People and places flickered through my memory's eye. I thought about every person, every place, and every animal I ever knew. I thought of everything but how to get myself off the almost full throttle train.

Ben grew smaller with my every blink. He was running fast as he could waving and hollering, "Ociee, get off! Get off NOW!"

"I can't!"

"You're gonna get your chicken self killed! JUMP!"

"BEN!" I swallowed hard. One foot loosed itself, then the other. Squeezing shut my eyes, I screamed, "Here I come!"

I leapt for the weed-covered bank.

The train's whistle sounded, *WOOOOO, Woo*!

Head first. I landed hard. I shook my head and spotted our horse, Maud. No wait, it wasn't Maud, it was Old Horse.

"Aren't you dead, Old Horse?"

Sure he was. Hadn't I cried for hours when Aunt Mamie wrote to tell me they'd put him down? Yet, there he was. Old Horse, plain as day, stood contentedly grazing in the shade of an oak tree.

"Old Horse, how'd you get here? Where's Mr. Lynch? Surely he wouldn't leave you all by yourself?"

A familiar voice called out to me. "Ociee, dearest."

"Mama? *Mama*!"

I couldn't believe I was seeing her! Mama looked so pretty, exactly like she did in the Gypsy's painted picture, the one I had carried with me to North Carolina and home again to Abbeville.

Mama came closer. Tangled in tall weeds, I couldn't move a finger. Was I frozen, not only my feet, but my entire body as well? Frozen? How could it be? The spring afternoon was toasty warm.

Mama smiled. I always loved her cheery face. When her lips parted to reveal white, shining teeth, Mama's eyes twinkled.

"You're not hurt, Ociee. I'm proud of you for being brave. Even so, my child, it's best not to be so daring."

"Yes, Mama. I'll be more careful."

Not hurt? I still couldn't walk to my mama. How I yearned to curl up in her arms. Was she keeping the truth from me? Were my legs gone? I heard about a train chopping a Marshall County man half in two.

"Come get me, Mama. Please, I need you!"

But my mama, our mama, was dead. She was dead like Old Horse. Measles took her away from us. She'd been gone for so long, too long, how long? Three years long. Why would a bunch of horrid red spots attack a person important to us?

"Mama?"

My loving, living Mama drifted away like a summer's cloud.

"Ociee!"

I blinked my eyes, trying desperately to hold them open. Like the rest of my body, they wouldn't cooperate.

"Please, Ociee, please wake up!"

My lips moved, but I swallowed my words.

"I'm going for Papa. I'll run like the wind to Fitch's."

My brother's panic washed over me like cold water. "Wait!"

"What? Ociee, did you say something? Please tell me you're not dead!"

"Don't know."

Cold and trembling, I wobbled my head. It felt full of fresh-picked cotton. I raised one hand to my face; the other still clutched Mama's locket. I rubbed my eyes. "What, what happened?"

Ben knelt down beside me. "Are you all right?"

I slowly sat up, brushing off weeds and dirt. What a relief, my legs were attached! I wiggled my toes. Rolling my shoulders, I rounded my neck back and forth. The cotton emptied from my head. "You get me into more trouble."

"Ociee, you're back!"

"Seems I am, no thanks to you, Ben Nash."

"I'm sorry."

"I know you are, Ben, you always are. I'll only forgive you if you tell Papa this was *your* idea."

"Guess I should."

I nodded.

"Ociee, I gotta tell you, girl, your jump was amazing! You leapt out so far you looked like a crow trying to escape from Tiger. Then *BAM*, down you went, head first. You crumpled up like an old rotted scarecrow!" He lowered his head. "At first I thought you'd died."

I shuddered. "Now I know what dead feels like."

"You do?"

"Maybe, but I don't feel like telling you."

"You're mad. I don't blame you. Hey, can you stand up?"

Ben attempted to steady me. We both wanted to believe I wasn't hurt.

"Can't do it. I'm dizzy."

As I tried to gather myself, Ben paced about fretting and watching and wringing his hands. Finally, he quieted and sat next to me.

"Any better?"

Once my brother settled himself, I got calmer.

"Think so. Ben, there's something I gotta tell you. Mama came to me."

"Mama? When?"

"When I hit the ground." I pointed toward the meadow. "She was standing over there. Everything in me wanted to touch her, Ben, but I couldn't move. She watched over me, the same way she did when I had the terrible fever. Mama was misty, as if she was covered with the lace on the parlor windows."

"Was she a ghost?"

"No, Ben, not a ghost. There wasn't anything scary about her. She was more like an angel. No, not an angel. It was our Mama, the same Mama she's always been."

"I don't believe you."

"I'm not sure I believe me either. But wait, Mama said something. She warned me not to be daring."

"Sounds like her."

"Yes, it does. I saw Old Horse, too."

"Mr. Lynch's horse?"

"Yes."

"Ociee, he's dead. You cried. Don't you remember?"

"He was here."

Ben, undoubtedly eager to make fun of my crazy talk about Old Horse, gave in to his more tender nature because he understood. During the time I was living in Asheville, North Carolina, our beloved pet Gray Dog passed away. Papa told me losing our dog had just about killed my brother.

We had been raised to understand such things. Through the years, when Mama and Papa, Ben, me, and our older brother Fred lived on our farm in Abbeville, chickens, ducks, even pigs, goats, and cows would get sick and die. Papa always taught us, "We farmers must learn to expect losses. Our task is to go on living with courage and with hope."

What we did not expect, however, was for Mama to die. I still get real mad about that. I'm not mad at our mama, not anymore. But I can't help boiling up at those dern measles for tearing apart our family.

I wasn't allowed to say 'dern.'

From time to time, Papa tried to assure us Mama wasn't really dead. He said she was in a better place. Heaven. He insisted we'd be with her again.

"My Bertie was such a perfect woman the Lord needed her more than do we."

I wasn't absolutely convinced our papa saw eye to eye with the Good Lord and His timing. What I do know is when I jumped from the train our mama came to check on me. I only wish she had stayed longer.

Ben patted my shoulder. "You feel like walking home, Ociee? Papa will be getting back soon. We're supposed to be there."

I stood up. "I'm feeling better. Let's go. Ben, I KNOW Mama was here."

"Or maybe, Ociee, you have a big hole in your head. Stop, let me take a look."

"Get your dirty hands out of my hair. I did so see Mama."

"I reckon." He kicked a rock on the dirt path. "I'm sorry."

"You should be, Ben, I could have been hurt."

"No, Ociee, I'm sorry about Mama. I wish real bad I'd seen her."

"I know."

As I thought back on the afternoon, I remembered smelling Mama's lavender, her sweet scent. I'd never lose that memory of her. Sometimes I'd scratch a tiny piece from a bar of lavender soap and put it under my nose. It brought comfort.

Maybe Mama came down from Heaven to cushion my fall. Perhaps she wanted to check on me like earthbound mamas do for their children. Old Horse was there, too, whether Ben believed me or not. Whatever happened, I was pleased they both appeared, if only for a few seconds.

I was also relieved I didn't break my leg or injure anything else because I was scheduled to return to Asheville in a few days. I didn't want to disappoint my Aunt Mamie. She'd be upset.

I wasn't about to admit it to Ben, but I was actually grateful he hoisted me onto the train.

I had one great ride!

Chapter 2

My adventure was far from the first time a Nash had leapt aboard a moving freight train. Our big brother Fred had done it all the time, at least, before he started courting his bride, Rebecca. He'd hop on, ride a mile, and jump off.

Returning home, Fred would refuse to share a single detail of his daring feat with Ben and me unless we pledged our total silence. Keeping secrets from our parents concerned me, but not for long.

"I was riding on a thunderbolt!" said Fred. "I could feel the tracks throbbing under me. Like being in an earthquake, tremors shot from the soles of my boots to the top of my head. My hat blew off with such force, it almost flew to Holly Springs."

After Rebecca came into his life, Fred pretty much walked around holding her hand and blushing. For a time, our brother clean forgot how to have any fun. At the same time, his passion for trains intensified. He discovered a grown man's way to be around trains; my brother went to work for the Illinois Central Railroad. His new job took him to Memphis, Tennessee.

Well before Fred got girl-goofy and started working for the railroad, he, Ben, and I regularly took peaches down to the tracks. We'd wait for the southbound train from Waterford, where it stopped to take on water. As it made its way towards Abbeville, we'd stand ready with a sack of peaches for the engineer. Soon as we heard the train's whistle, we started hollering to wave it down.

"Look there!"

"Here it comes!"

"The engineer's leaning out, he must see us!"

The boys liked to spot the man shoveling coal into the hot, fiery engine. I was partial to the caboose, my favorite car. The caboose was red and different from the others. Like me, it was the last car in line.

Once in a while, I'd notice a hobo man peeking out from inside a boxcar. Even though hobos scared me plenty, I was as brave as an army soldier standing with my brothers.

Because Fred was much older than us, he'd insist on handing off the sack to the engineer.

"Too risky for you two," he'd say.

I didn't care as much as Ben, who always frowned at Fred.

*

After Fred began his career with the Illinois Central Railroad, we learned many interesting facts from him. One piece of information was particularly disturbing. Seems we weren't special after all. Fred told us train folks often received gifts of food from farmers. I preferred to think we Nashes were uniquely generous folks. So, even with my excellent memory, I tried to make my smart self forget what Fred said.

According to my brother, there was a disgusting motto, something else I was happier not knowing. He quoted an old engineer, "My boy, peaches always taste better at night."

"Why, sir?"

"Because it's dark, you can't see the worms you're eating."

Ben laughed.

I about vomited.

Anybody with sense would know our peaches would never host a slimy worm. Not Papa's. He was the best farmer ever, even though we did lose our farm. It wasn't due to Papa's lack of skill. After Mama died, he discovered he was better suited to working at Fitch's Mercantile.

As Aunt Mamie said, "George Nash is cut out to be a

city person."

So was I. I discovered my city mindset during my months with her in the big town of Asheville, North Carolina. That said, being home in Mississippi for the past few weeks had unquestionably brought back the country girl in me.

I was a person who was *adaptable*, a word Aunt Mamie taught me. It meant I could make myself comfortable in more than one situation. I'd make a point to include my thoughts about the country and the city in my journal. I'd have to admit I had NOT been very *adaptable* riding the flatcar. I was cross-eyed terrified!

*

"Ociee, you're a mess! You're covered in dirt and weeds," said Papa. "What have you two gotten into now?"

I wanted to believe we were going to be perfectly honest with Papa. His reaction convinced me all the more. Ben was supposed to speak first. Yet there he stood, gazing out the kitchen window looking as spotless as fresh fallen snow.

"Nothing much, Papa," I said, glaring at Ben. I shook my head, brushing away the rubble. "See, I licked the blood right off my arm. Don't want you to worry, not for a minute."

"Ociee."

Ben finally opened his mouth, "Papa, I promised I'd be the one to tell. I hoisted Ociee up on a flatcar. It was going slow, at first, anyway. She rode only a short piece."

Ben put his arm around me. "You can see for yourself, my sister here is fine as she can be."

Papa took off his hat, ran his fingers through his hair and sighed. We knew we were in for a talking to.

"Papa, there's one more thing," I added. "I saw Mama."

"Ociee, darlin' girl. You know better . . . "

Before he could finish, I got upon a stool to go eyeball to eyeball with him. "I did, Papa, I did see her. Mama came down from Heaven, sure as sunshine, right after I jumped."

Again, Papa quieted. When he looked that serious we

understood to stand stick still and be extra quiet.

"We've had this talk so many times, too many times, children. I'm not talking about your mama; I am talking about you two doing dangerous things. Now, sit yourselves down."

Ben and I slid into our seats at the kitchen table. He sat at the head. I began to roll the hem of the red checked tablecloth between my fingertips.

Papa continued, "It's not only this incident, Ben, Ociee. I well remember the unsafe contraption you three built using the cart's old wheels and the apple box. Wasn't it Fred who greased the timbers with lard and sent Ociee whizzing down from the top of the smokehouse?"

"Since we're telling truths," said Ben, "I helped."

"Papa, I was pleased the boys asked me to play, honored they let me go first. I'm every bit as brave as my brothers."

"Lord, have mercy."

"But I liked it, Papa! I didn't get a scratch."

"Ociee, just like today, you could have been badly hurt. No one in this family ever stops to consider such. Makes me wonder how Fred would do were he and Rebecca to have a child."

I swallowed hard. I hadn't thought about any babies. I was still getting accustomed to my brother being a husband.

Papa cleared his throat. The sound startled me.

"I'll never forget the day you and Ben chased after the Gypsy man." Papa rolled his eyes. "Running from him almost cost you your mama's locket."

"Papa, that Gypsy wasn't one bit mean like Fred told us Gypsies were. Remember, he said they boil children in big pots! Our Gypsy was kindhearted. Why, if he hadn't found Mama's locket, I wouldn't have it today."

I pulled the tiny golden heart from under my shirt. He only came in our house because he wanted to return this to me. Hold on, I'm gonna get his painting of Mama."

"Sit down."

I folded my arms across my chest.

"Ociee, I'm thankful the man found your locket, and I appreciate his art," said Papa. "It's a good likeness of your mama."

"And of her smile."

Papa closed his eyes. "Yes, Ociee, her sweet smile."

He opened his eyes and took my hand. Looking at me and at Ben, Papa said, "Let the Gypsy's painting serve as a reminder for you to never judge a person by his manner of dress or by what others say about him. This includes any tales Fred might tell. Look for what's worthy in people. There might be a reason someone is the way he is."

"Yes, Papa. Fred sure was wrong about the Gypsy."

"Likely your brother was only trying to get a rise out of you."

"Fred's terrific at rising me," laughed Ben.

Papa didn't respond. He seemed edgy. A chill ran through my body. Had another bad thing happened?

"You well remember how thrilled we were when Ociee came home for Fred's wedding." Papa turned toward me. "My darling girl, you must realize your months in Asheville were lonesome for the boys and me. And, as beneficial as your time with Aunt Mamie turned out to be, it was hardest for you."

"I know, Papa, but I'll be better when I go back."

"That's my girl." Papa drifted off. "It felt so right having us all here."

"Papa, I wrote about it in my journal! You wished you could stop the hands on your pocket watch so's to keep us together. There we were, you, Fred, Ben and me riding in our wagon with Maud pulling us home. Papa, don't you want me to get my journal? I could read your exact words."

"No, Ociee. But thank you. It's good for you to keep records of important things."

"I learned from you, Papa. I watch you write at your desk."

Ben piped up, "I don't like writing. Too much like school. Don't like nothing about it."

"*Anything*, son, you don't like *anything* about it."

Papa's years at the University of North Carolina would show up from time to time, specifically when he talked about serious matters. His interest in education was about to take hold again.

"Not true, Ben," I said. "You know you delight in telling stories."

"It's the *telling* I like, Ociee, not the *writing*. Takes too much time to write. Besides, I'm busy doing important things." He grinned and readied himself to make mischief. I knew well that expression. He leaned toward me, "You know, Ociee, like pushing my silly sister onto a train!"

I leapt up. "*Silly sister*, am I?" I went for him. Papa grabbed me around my waist and sat me down.

"Enough out of you two. I have something to say, and you children are making it nearly impossible. Ociee Nash, Ben Nash, behave!"

Papa used a stern teacher tone. Then he was silent and stayed so for several minutes. Worry crawled up and down my back.

Papa hadn't seemed extremely upset about our train antics. Ben and I had done worse. Even while he was scolding us, I wanted to believe he admired my courage. Something was sure enough wrong though. Our papa was postponing his discussion as much as he said we were. He walked to the window.

Ben fiddled with the bowl of daises I'd arranged earlier. It was one time I didn't fuss at him. More minutes passed. Ben and I eyed one another. Again I started fingering the hem of the tablecloth.

Was his concern something else with me or with Ben?

Was it about Fred and Rebecca? Had my mentioning Mama troubled him? Or could it have been his job at Fitch's Mercantile? Aunt Mamie? Mamie!

"Papa, are you upset because I'm going back to North Carolina?"

Papa seated himself, putting his hands together like he was getting ready to pray. His back stiffened.

"No, Ociee, the fact is the plans have changed. Please trust what I'm going to say is for the best. You both know full well our family is what matters most to me."

"Papa!" Ben shouted. "I'm going to Asheville instead of Ociee!" Ben knocked over his chair and began to skip around the kitchen. He was shouting and clapping his hands. "It's my turn! Ociee's staying here, and I'm going to North Carolina. Hoorah for me!"

I sat hushed as stone.

"For patience sakes, son, calm yourself! No one's going to Mamie's. You, Ociee, and I are moving to Memphis, Tennessee."

Ben righted his chair and plopped down.

My bottom jaw dropped to my chest as concern turned into disbelief. I could see into my room. My traveling hat, perched on the bedpost, waited to be worn. I wasn't going to Asheville. I bit my lip.

"You all right, Ociee?" said Papa.

"Yes, sir," I replied with a sniff.

"Papa, what about Tiger?" said Ben, "I have to take him with me. I won't go if they don't allow cats in Memphis!"

"Of course, cats are allowed in Memphis. Now, *carrying* Tiger all the way to Tennessee is another story. I don't know how you'll manage such a feat, but you are welcome to try."

Ben stood at the back door. "Here, Tiger!"

Tiger was nowhere to be found, but Ben was only

pretending to hunt for his cat. Papa's announcement shocked my brother the same way it did me. He was trying to untangle his feelings.

"Come here, boy. I'm sorry you're upset, but we're moving again."

We surely hadn't given our papa the enthusiastic response he'd expected. I was sniffling. Ben was hollering. Papa stood up with his hands held high over his head. I thought about the picture of Moses in my Sunday school book, the one where Moses parts the Red Sea. I felt more like one of Pharaoh's soldiers when the sea flooded back and they were washed away, chariots and all.

I half expected Mama to appear again. I inhaled, hoping for her lavender. No scent came.

Chapter 3

"Children, you best get comfortable."

When I was nine years old and Papa talked to me about me moving to Asheville to live with Aunt Mamie, I tried hard to understand. It didn't work. I was hoping being eleven would make things easier.

He began, "Ociee, you're observant. You notice how I write every night."

"Yes, Papa, you're working on the ledgers for Mr. Fitch."

"Usually, but lately I've also been studying through a correspondence course. Keep your seats, I'll be back."

Papa left us alone at the kitchen table. Knowing how serious he was, Ben and I stared at one another, saying not a word. He returned from the parlor with a large book. He put in the center of our table. The word *Draughons* was on the cover.

"This is what I'm doing, I'm taking a business course."

"Papa, I thought you already knew everything about business. Mrs. Fitch told me you're such a smart man you made their store run better than ever."

"I'm glad you hold such a lofty opinion of me, sweet girl."

"Studying, Papa?" Ben couldn't believe what he was hearing. "Why would a full-grown man do school work when he didn't have to?"

Papa ruffled my brother's hair. "Hopefully, Ben Nash, one of these days you will turn your mind in the direction of study. You might find it useful. A man's success is often judged by his knowledge."

Ben shrugged his shoulders.

I smiled. "Papa, you know our Ben. He's counting on discovering a gold mine. Once he finds a proper mule, he'll be heading out west."

"And I'll be taking Tiger with me."

"I suppose dreams of going west are in your blood, my boy."

Ben puffed up like a rooster.

Papa reared back in his chair. "When word came Joseph Nash left his land to Mamie and me, your mama and I made our own westward journey."

Any time Papa talked about their early years, his memories brought brightness to his face. It was on the farm outside Abbeville, we were born, first Fred, then Ben, and last, me. Papa reminisced about working the land, their fruit orchards, their bountiful vegetable garden bursting with corn stalks, tomato and bean vines, squash, peas and turnips. Papa stared through Ben and me, as if he could wish himself back to those sunshine days.

I mentioned what I treasured most, our cozy frame house. "Remember our magical front porch and how we could sit on the wood swing and call up the roundest moon and the brightest stars?"

"It's true," said Ben. "Every evening, the moon came up just for the Nashes!"

Papa nodded. "Indeed it did, for us alone."

"I miss our pigs and cows even with all the work they put on me," added Ben.

Papa chuckled.

I perked up. "I loved our horses. We'll be able to ride in Memphis, won't we, Papa?"

"Yes, of course, Ociee. Maud will be relieved to carry you instead of the heavy wagonload she'll haul getting us there."

"I'll be riding her, too," said Ben. "I'll still miss our pets, Papa, Gray Dog, most of all. Ociee says Mama is caring for him in Heaven. Is it true?"

"Ociee's absolutely right," said Papa.

I nearly cried, realizing Maud was our last surviving animal.

"I remember Mama's flowers, too, specially the daylilies and the daisies, the ones I helped plant."

Suddenly grief robbed the color from our papa's face. He stopped paying attention to our conversation. The familiar sadness about Mama and our farm hit me next, then Ben.

Papa stood up, returning the book to his desk. "Supper's cold. Ociee, Ben, we'd best eat."

We ate quietly until Papa spoke up. His own gloom lifted as he said, "I want you two to consider our move as an adventure. Ben, it can be the first miles you travel toward your gold mine."

"Yes, siree!"

"Don't be forgetting the reason we're moving is to bring together our family." Papa was good at turning people's doubts to hope. "I know you children have heard about the Mississippi River. It cuts in two the whole of America as it runs from way up north in Minnesota all the way down to the Gulf of Mexico. Memphis is one of the largest ports on the river. All manner of boats and barges, riverboats, too, dock day and night in our new town."

"I know about those riverboats from Miss Brown, my teacher," Ben said. "She showed us pictures. Riverboats have these great big paddle wheels to push them up and down the river! Fine folks get to ride on 'em, even get to sleep on 'em, too. Do you think I could become a captain? Can't you see Tiger and me running a riverboat!"

"First you insist on subjecting Tiger to a long wagon trip. Now you want to put the poor cat on a riverboat. Son, don't you know cats hate water?"

"Tiger really will have a hard time in the wagon?"

"I'm afraid so, son. Your cat likes his territory; he's accustomed to roaming free. The travel will be tough enough for us, but fearsome for Tiger. This is your decision, Ben. You have permission to take him, IF you can accept the responsibility."

Ben hung his head.

*

I'd had enough change in my life. I couldn't sleep for tossing in my feather bed. I saw the faces of the people I loved, those dead and those living: Papa, Mama, my brothers, Rebecca, Aunt Mamie, the Gypsy man, and my friends in Asheville. They flitted in and out of my mind like thousands of fireflies.

*

I was eight when Mama died, nine when I was sent away. Papa thought my Aunt Mamie's influence was what I needed. I did NOT agree. The thought of riding by myself on a big noisy train had scared the breath out of me. Far worse, I was deeply distressed to leave behind my family. When I said goodbye to Papa, to Fred, and Ben, they had to peel me off. But, as Papa said, Aunt Mamie had a caring nature, and everything turned out well. I met wonderful people, including Elizabeth Murphy, my very best friend besides Ben. She lived down the street from my aunt.

Elizabeth! Oh my soul, I'd have to write her and try to explain why I wasn't coming back. How could I? I twisted and turned and got tangled in my bed sheet. An owl hooted. "Hush up, you owl. Don't you be upsetting me about leaving. I'll be fine, you'll see."

I wasn't telling the owl the truth.

While I was living in Asheville, Papa came to visit. I nearly burst I was so thrilled. Sadly, our reunion turned to tears when he told me he'd sold our farm. I pitched such a hissy, I lost Mama's locket for the second time.

Thankfully, I found it, and on my own.

Losing our farm had been a dreadful disappointment for our papa, but I was grieving mostly for myself. I wouldn't understand Papa's regret until I was grown. He carried his hurt nearly as deeply as he bore the loss of his beloved Bertie. I squeezed shut my eyes and envisioned Mama's tombstone.

Susan Alberta M. "Bertie" Nash, 1853–1897
Beloved wife of George W. Nash

I eventually drifted off to sleep.

*

Papa left the next morning in a borrowed buggy. He traveled to Memphis to visit Fred and Rebecca and set up things for our move. For us Nashes, our lives either dragged slow as cold honey or fast as lightning flashes. Reading my journal, I saw that during the past two years we'd turned from honey people into a thunderbolt family.

Mrs. Fitch came to stay with Ben and me, even though he and I argued we'd be safe as bugs in rugs by ourselves. We hadn't earned back our papa's trust.

"If I'm to feel welcome in your home, I'll have to change my name," said Mrs. Fitch. "From this day forward, I am 'Mrs. Adelaide'."

"Yes, ma'am, Mrs. Adelaide."

She and Mama had been close friends. Anytime we went into Abbeville to purchase fabric, thread, flour, salt and the like, she and Mama shared a pot of tea and visited. Mrs. Adelaide and I had our own lady kind of closeness, too. It began a few weeks prior, when I found a box buried under a rosebush at our old farm. Papa believed the treasure inside rightfully belonged to me, but wanted Homer Fitch's opinion. I was made to sit with Mrs. Fitch while the men discussed MY find. I was livid! Mrs. Fitch set my mind at ease.

"Ociee, I think Bertie guided you, her precious daughter,

to that treasure."

It was then I knew I trusted her the same way Mama had.

Thanks to Mrs. Adelaide's doing the cooking and the woman's work, I had time to get organized. First, I'd write Elizabeth. She was going to be mad as a hot hornet. I planned to write Aunt Mamie next but there wasn't a rush. She already knew about Memphis because Papa sent her a telegram. My aunt must have been awfully sad about the change of plans. I could almost see her standing in my empty bedroom dabbing tears from her eyes. To Aunt Mamie I was her own little girl.

> *My dear Elizabeth,*
>
> *If you want to shoot a person, please do not shoot me. I am simply obeying Papa. Our family is moving to Memphis, Tennessee. The good news is Tennessee is the state next to North Carolina. It is not as far away as Mississippi. The other good news is my whole family will be living in the same town.*
>
> *What I am so, so, so sad about is I will not be living in Asheville with Aunt Mamie where I can be with you, my very best girl friend in the world. I promised you I would come back. Elizabeth, I even had my ticket and my trunk packed. Please forgive me. Mark my words, I will come one of these days.*
>
> *As soon as we get to Memphis, I will send you a note with our address. Do you like being a pen-friend with me? I like it, too. Please begin a letter telling me all about our friends and our school and*

anything else you think of.

I give you permission to have a new best friend, but please let me always be a special friend. You can be my dearest North Carolina person, while I will be your dearest Tennessee person.

I've been working on this letter for hours. I must stop. I will write you again soon.

I miss you, Elizabeth BEST NORTH CAROLINA FRIEND Murphy,

Yours always, Ociee Nash of Mississippi, North Carolina and Tennessee

Mrs. Adelaide was sweet to Ben. She referred to him by his given name, 'Benjamin.' Usually grown folks only use "givens" when children misbehave. Mrs. Adelaide called him Benjamin because Mama loved his name.

"Benjamin, I adore cats. Your Tiger has won a spot in my heart."

Pouring a saucer of milk, she sat to string green beans. "Come here, little kitty, here's your treat."

Ben joined her. "Need some help with the beans?"

"Why, yes, Benjamin!"

Ben looked at Tiger sadly. "I got something to ask you."

*

When Papa returned from his trip to Memphis, I raced to greet him.

"Ociee, girl!"

"Papa!" The best part about folks leaving is welcoming them home.

Mrs. Adelaide came out, her bag packed. "George Nash, your children were angels, but my Homer is anxious for me to get home." She gave me a hug and again told Papa how well behaved we were.

He acted like he wasn't surprised, but he was. He picked me up and whirled me in circles until I got dizzy. It was my best dizzy ever. Ben was playing a game of hoops a street over. I had Papa all to myself.

"Sure am proud of you and Ben. I hope you'll keep up this behavior."

"We will, Papa. You weren't gone any time. I hardly got around to missing you, but I'm pretty sure I did."

He squeezed me to him.

"Tell me about Fred. They've only been gone a couple of weeks, but seems like they've been in Memphis forever."

"Fred and '*Mae*' are doing perfectly fine."

"Who's Mae? What happened to Rebecca?"

I was horrified. Had my brother changed wives?

"Gracious goodness, Ociee. I meant no such thing! 'Mae' is Fred's pet name for Rebecca. A husband often calls his wife by something other than her given name."

"I know Papa said 'Bertie' for Mama's Alberta."

"Correct, or like your 'Ociee.' Your name came from Ben's struggle to say 'Josie,' short for Josephine. Guess I got in a habit of calling Rebecca by *Mae* because I heard Fred say it so often."

"You're fooling me, Papa, you know you said 'Mae' because you wanted to watch my face drop."

"You caught me, Ociee, and what a funny face you made!"

I liked when Papa made jokes.

"Mae's given name is Rebecca Mae Hutchinson. She kept putting Fred's proposals off with a 'maybe' so after they married, your brother shortened her 'maybe' to May, spelled M-a-e."

"I'll have to get used to it. I like Rebecca, but I want her to pick. Did you know Mr. Fitch's wife changed her name? She told us to call her Mrs. Adelaide."

"How gracious. I'll remain 'Papa.' I hope you'll always

be my Ociee."

"I'll always be your Ociee."

Ben trotted up. I grinned at him. "Papa's home, I saw him first."

Ben looked up at Papa eagerly. "Did you see the riverboats?"

"And hello to you, son."

"Sorry, Papa. Welcome home, now, about the riverboats."

"I did, and once we get settled, I plan to take you down to the Mississippi. Maybe let you go aboard one."

"Hoorah! Papa, do you think Fred might leave the railroad and join up with me?"

"Not likely, Ben. In fact, your hardworking brother is close to making fireman."

"Fireman!" Ben and I chanted in unison. "What about the Illinois Central?"

"Fred has always wanted to be an engineer. Why would he leave to fight fires?" I asked, "Besides it's awful dangerous work. Our wonderful Fred might get burned to a crisp!"

"Slow down! Fred is doing so well, his superior is moving him up to become a fireman, a fireman for the *railroad*. Your brother is very young to have accomplished this much."

"Hooray for Fred Nash," we chanted.

I couldn't resist. "Fred's married to Mae."

Oblivious, Ben said, "When does he start being a fireman?"

*

I'd never seen our papa so full of life. He'd set up his schooling with Draughons and found us a home, a mix of our farmhouse and the one in Abbeville. Best of all, it had a front porch. I prayed we'd be able to see the moon. He also arranged to borrow Mr. Fitch's extra horse and wagon.

"We'll either drive for one horribly long day," said Papa, "or cut the trip in half and camp out along the way."

"Camp out!"

"No, Ben, keep going," I pleaded. "I don't want to wake up in the woods sticky and wet the next morning." I had to admit it. I was definitely becoming girlish.

We watched Papa as he unpacked. "By the way, there is another surprise. Can either of you guess what it might be?"

"Something about riverboats?"

"No! For goodness sakes, Ben, can you think of nothing else?"

Ben frowned.

"No, Papa, he can't. Unless, he's back to going west on his mule."

Papa laughed so hard I got tickled, too.

Ben scowled harder. "Don't make fun of me!"

"I'm not, son. Actually, the joke is on us, on Ociee and me. You see I've discovered a number of facts about our new hometown. You might be glad to learn, along with cotton and lumber, our town boasts a tremendous mule trade."

"Mule trade?"

"That's right, son. Memphis is the mule capital of the South."

Ben Nash was speechless.

Papa continued, "Now I have an announcement."

"What, Papa?"

He tilted his head to the side, and breathing in, announced, "Fred wanted to surprise you, but I can't wait. Tomorrow night, your brother will catch a ride on the southbound train and help us move! He's going to drive our second wagon to Memphis."

"Papa, this is gonna be the grandest trip!"

Ben was unhappy. "But I wanted to drive. I practiced with Maud."

"Don't fret, Ben, Fred may let you take over the reins. After all, it's quite a journey. It took me longer to get to Memphis by buggy than it took for your sister to go all the way to Asheville."

Ben and I got riled up. "Why can't WE ride the train?"

Ben was mad because he long yearned for an honest-to-goodness train trip. For me, I was becoming spoiled. Not only would the train have been faster, but also we wouldn't have to sleep on the ground.

Papa shook his head. "For one thing, we must get our possessions to Memphis."

"I know, Papa, I could tote Mama's crystal vase, her portrait and colored bottles on the train, AND her quilts and crocheted pieces, too. I can sit on anything cloth. I took her prettiest quilt to North Carolina and took care of it, too."

"I know you did, Ociee. I'm depending on your help, particularly with your mama's things. She would appreciate how much her treasures mean to her daughter."

I beamed. To me, being a 'daughter' was akin to being a princess.

My brother argued. "We could take anything we needed on the dern train."

"Ben Nash, don't be saying 'dern.' Now, I suppose you'd plan to hold our kitchen table on your lap along with the CAT?"

"I could."

"After a few hours the oak table would get unbelievably heavy. Walk around our house and make your own list. The only way to get our furniture, our cooking things, dishes, linens and clothes to Memphis is by wagon."

"I know, Papa. I just *need* a real train ride."

"I promise, Ben, one of these days, you will get your wish."

"You promise?"

"You have my solemn word."

"All right then."

Ben went out to feed Maud, and I suppose, to discuss our journey with her. I excused myself to finish up in my room. Papa came in, and reaching into his pocket, said, "Here's a letter for Miss Ociee Nash."

Lovely white stationery, black ink; her handwriting was perfectly formed and artistic, like a queen's might be. I could almost smell the gardenias in Aunt Mamie's summer garden.

Papa clicked his tongue. "I'll see what I can put together to eat. You and Ben have been spoiled by Adelaide's good cooking."

I could hear him whistling as he looked around the kitchen. "Wait a song bird's second. Adelaide left us supper!"

Apprehensive, I opened the letter.

> *My darling Ociee,*
>
> *I cannot imagine how thrilled you are to be moving to Memphis, where your entire family will be together once and for all. I well remember how you missed everyone during the precious few months I had you with me.*
>
> *I now know you rather well, my dear. I fear you might be concerned I am disappointed you are not returning to 66 Charlotte Street. I am writing to you before you get yourself worked into a tizzy. Please trust that I am abundantly happy for you, my child. I am also happy for my dear brother George and for your brothers.*
>
> *You are not to worry one moment about me. I may have some excitement of my own, but shall wait and confirm my announcement until you and yours are well settled into your new home.*

As of late, you have not shared any comments with me about reading. Should I be concerned you are not taking time for books? Please, dear child, do schedule reading after your trip.

I often see Elizabeth Murphy and her lovely parents. My dear Ociee, you and Elizabeth must attempt to remain devoted friends, no matter the miles between you. I strongly suggest you stay in contact through letter writing.

I wish for you and your beloved family a safe and pleasant journey.

With my love, Aunt Mamie Nash

Aunt Mamie was right. I'd not been reading, not the first word. Was my aunt watching from the top of the Blue Ridge Mountains? I was also worried about hurting her feelings. Thank glory Papa sent her the telegram so I wasn't the one breaking the news. I'd put off writing her. How like Aunt Mamie to make things easier for me. She would be pleased that I wrote Elizabeth.

Chapter 4

After we ate Mrs. Adelaide's sliced ham, tomatoes, beans, cornbread, and blueberry pie, Ben and I did dishes without acting ornery. Our good behavior continued. In my view, Ben's fussing about the train did not count.

I kissed Papa on his cheek, washed up, and put on my nightclothes. Wiggling down into my bed, I wrapped up in Mama's quilt

For a butterfly's blush, I sniffed lavender.

*

I was so worked up; I awakened well before the sun. I'd never traveled with my whole family, before. Papa was excited, too. I found him sorting out things and whistling again. It wasn't an actual tune, but more a cheerful tweeting sound.

"Good morning, Papa."

"Good morning to you, Ociee. Sorry to act startled; I didn't expect you up early."

He attempted to hide an odd-shaped box, one with two latches.

"What do you have there, Papa?"

"Nothing to interest you. Why don't you see about breakfast? There's fresh sausage. I have a hankering for eggs and sausage. Don't you?"

Papa wasn't getting off easy. "What's the strange box? I saw you slide it behind your trunk. Are you trying to hide something? Please, Papa, I want to see."

"Well, if you must, Miss Nosey." He snapped open the latches. The case, lined in faded green velvet, smelled of mildew. He pulled back the fabric and revealed an old wooden fiddle, one like Mr. Watts played at Fred's wedding.

"All right, Ociee, you've seen my secret. How about breakfast?"

"Where'd it come from?"

"I brought it from North Carolina."

"North Carolina?"

"Sure did."

"I remember when you played your harmonica, but who played this fiddle?"

"Your papa, I'm ashamed to admit." He held the fiddle as gently as he would a baby kitten. "I haven't touched this thing since Ben was born. Got busy farming and loving my family."

"Sweet Papa."

"I came upon this fiddle one other time," he said. "When we moved from the farm to this house. Can't decide whether to take it to Memphis."

"You have to! Will you play it for me? Papa, please play the fiddle."

Sitting down on his bed, Papa carefully lifted the fiddle from the case. He was tender as he dusted it and tightened the strings.

Pling, plunk, ping. "Not too bad a sound after my neglect. Needs attention to these strings." Putting it down, Papa brought the bow close to his face examining it. "Good. No bow bugs."

"Bow bugs?"

"Yep, see these horse hairs along the bow?"

I scooted up closer to Papa. "Yes."

"If you're not careful, bow bugs get in and have a feast."

"I'm mighty glad the taste of yours didn't appeal to hungry bugs."

I was being serious, but Papa laughed. He picked up the fiddle, and putting it under his chin, he took the bow in his right hand. "These horse hairs make the sounds sweet and melodic. Listen."

He drew the bow back and forth across the strings. As Papa began to play, I was scooped up and placed on the banks of a bubbling creek. The sounds of soft wind and birdsong filled the room.

"Papa, it's beautiful!" I swooned, "Your fiddle brings music from outside in."

"Thank you, Ociee, yours is generous praise, indeed. You have a way of making the plainest things sound impressive."

He held the instrument out and studied it. "To tell you the truth, I'm surprised this old fiddle plays as well as she does, given how long she's gone without care."

"*She*? You remember Mr. Charles, the train conductor who watched after me on my trip?"

"Yes, but what does Mr. Charles have to do with my fiddle?"

"You said, 'She's gone without care.' Mr. Charles also refers to trains, boats and other things that aren't people as *shes*. Papa, exactly what is it about your fiddle that makes it a *she*?"

Holding the fiddle upright for me to observe, he said, "Because she's shaped like a girl!"

"Papa!" I blushed.

He winked at me.

"Papa, play her again, play her for me!"

"Not yet, Ociee, we've got too much to do to be frittering away our time."

I knew not to press him.

He nodded at the fiddle. "By gum, I AM going to take her to Memphis. She'll need resin to shine her strings, but this old gal's still got music she yearns to share. Ociee, let's us get breakfast going."

Papa placed the fiddle in her case next to his trunk.

*

The music didn't wake Ben, but the frying sausage brought him to his feet. He loved breakfast. I did, too. Papa was sipping his second cup of coffee when we heard boots coming up the front steps.

"Good morning, Nashes. Any body home?"

"Fred! Fred! "Ben and I almost knocked over the table running to him.

Papa, cup in hand, followed, beaming brighter than the sun.

"This IS one happy scene. Welcome home, Fred. Don't you want some sausage and eggs before I put you to work?"

"I thought you'd never ask."

Ben and I each took one of Fred's hands and pulled him toward the kitchen.

"Are we planning on leaving tomorrow morning?"

"The sooner the better," said Papa. "I wouldn't mind leaving today."

"Today? I had a feeling you would. Suits me. I'm gone so bloomin' much with the railroad, my bride gets lonesome."

I was stunned, but too excited to complain. Besides, I'd been packed for days.

"Fred came sooner than I expected so it must be written in the stars for us to leave," said Papa. "But first, let's all sit around the table together. Your brother needs to catch his breath and eat a bite. Pass him the biscuits."

I grabbed for the biscuits, but Ben got to them first.

Fred smiled. "Thanks Ben. Have you grown since I saw you last month?"

Ben sat ramrod straight. "I think so."

I stiffened my back. "Me, too, Fred."

"I'm not sure you're any bigger, Ociee. But you sure are turning into a pretty girl with your blond curls."

I made a face, half smiling, half not. I appreciated what he said, but I wanted to remain a bit of a boy. If I were too girlish, Ben would never let me play games with him. I shook my head to make my curls bounce.

Fred chuckled. He noticed lady things since he got married.

In a singsong voice I said, "So how is my new sister *Mae* doing?"

"Papa shared Rebecca's nickname with you, did he?"

Papa arched a brow. "Didn't think you'd mind, son."

"No, sir. You like it, Ociee?"

"I do."

"Doesn't matter to me," said Ben. "Call her whatever she likes. Can your wife bake cakes?"

"Yes, she can. You don't think Mrs. Hutchinson would send off her only child unless she could cook, do you?"

"Guess not, Fred. Reckon I'll call her Mae like everybody else does. It's quicker than saying Rebecca. 'Rebecca, will you please give me some cake?' Or, 'Mae, cake please.' I'll call her Mae."

Our papa seemed as content as if he were resting in the shade of a hickory tree by a pond with his fishing pole in one hand and a cool glass of lemonade in the other. He smiled about Ben and Mae's cake, turning his gaze from one of us to the other. Nothing in the world was troubling George Nash. He had his family back together.

Chapter 5

"The Mississippi River is huge, nearly as big as I used to believe the ocean to be," said Fred as he took a bite of sausage. "Day and night, Cobblestone Landing bustles with small boats, large vessels, barges loaded with timber and cotton, and paddlewheel riverboats. Memphis is a major port . . . "

"Riverboats!"

"Ben, don't interrupt Fred."

"It's all right, Ociee, everyone loves the riverboats. They feature decks, two and three stories high on both sides, which are filled with passengers chatting, singing, and dancing. Everyone on shore waves at the people on board, who are having the times of their lives. Music fills the air."

"Music. Papa, you could play your fiddle!"

"Now who's interrupting? Wait, what fiddle?"

"I'll tell you later, Ben."

"I do have a vague memory, Papa," said Fred. "I can almost recall you sitting on the back porch playing a tune for Mama and me."

"Son, please talk about Memphis, not about some long forgotten song."

"If you insist, but with these two, you're not off the hook. Where was I?"

"The Mississippi."

"You just have to see it for yourselves. But for now, close your eyes and imagine the evening sky. The river is like a slice of that sky but sprinkled with many, many boats instead of with hundreds of stars."

I could almost hear the Mississippi's water lapping against the cobblestones at the Memphis landing.

"Now, we can't get to the river without going through

downtown, but, because of the beautiful tall buildings, that's real exciting, too. We'll be sure to go by the Cotton Exchange, which is bigger than anything you've ever seen. Five years old, it's where the cotton merchants carry on their daily business. I tell you, Memphis is a remarkable place. Your eyes are gonna shoot out of their sockets."

"Don't eat, Fred. Keep talking," begged Ben.

"I can do both. Learned how on the railroad. Another building I'll show you is the Porter Building, the first steel-frame skyscraper in Memphis. I read it's the tallest building in the world to have its own hot water heating system."

I didn't care about heating. Fireplaces suited me. But 'skyscraper' got my attention. "The Porter scrapes the sky?"

Ben nearly leaped out of his chair. "Did you hear THAT, Papa? We're gonna see the tallest building in the world. I may burst!"

"I hope not, Ben, because if you burst," said Papa, "You'll miss the skyscraper."

Ben didn't bat an eye. The two of us studied Fred, trying to get our minds around every word he spoke.

"Ociee, I know you like to read. So does Mae, and she's planning to take you to the Cossitt Library. After her first visit there, she said you couldn't get to every book they offer even if you never left the building!"

"Mae likes books, too? Aunt Mamie will be pleased to learn we have something else in common."

"No books for me," said Ben, "but I'm sure gonna see the skyscraper!"

"When Papa came last week I took him for a ride around Front Street, Union, Monroe, Poplar, Main Street, and Madison Avenue. Where else, Papa?"

"I have no idea, son. I was too busy craning my neck to make notes."

"There are so many banks downtown, I heard a fellow refer to Madison Avenue, the heart of the city, as the 'Wall

Street of Memphis.'"

"Fred, you sound like a political man. I think the city fathers should hire you to encourage folks to move to Memphis."

"I'm already bringing one new family."

"Who?"

"He means US, Ben!"

"I knew that."

"When Fred rode me around, I couldn't count the number of fancy restaurants. Who eats in those places? You can't imagine the stores. Front windows display a king's ransom in jewelry and clothing."

"Who's the politician *now*, Papa?"

"Reckon it's me."

"Wait until you ride a streetcar."

"A CAR!" Ben shouted. He leapt up, knocking every plate off the table, along with Papa and Fred's coffees, the cream pitcher, and my half-finished milk. "I'm gonna ride in a CAR!"

"Good job, Ben."

"Didn't mean to."

"Not to worry. We'll have a few less dishes to carry," said Papa, as he willingly began to clean up the mess. No one offered to help, but he didn't seem to mind. We pushed our chairs to either side of Fred's and readied ourselves for more.

"Not a *car*, little brother, although there are a good many around. Streetcars, also called trolleys, run on tracks like trains. But they don't use coal, they have wires running them from overhead."

"Like magic," I said.

Papa emptied the broken dishes into the trash and said, "Like magic, Ociee. Like magic, Ben. Like MAGIC, I'm making you disappear. We're leaving!"

"What?"

"Hocus, pocus!" Papa waved his fork in the air. "Disappear to your rooms, strip your beds, gather your belongings, and slide your trunks into the hallway. While Fred and I load furniture and these boxes on the wagons, feed Maud. She's gonna need her breakfast."

"Yes sir!"

"Mr. Fitch will arrive any minute to drop off his wagon."

*

We were whirling in a tornado high up in the sky. Nevertheless, I wasn't afraid, not the least bit, because I wasn't alone. Papa, Fred, and Ben were riding with me in the giant twister.

An hour later, I tied tight my traveling hat, the one I always wore. My hat assured safety and good fortune whenever I went to a far away place, particularly to a place unknown to me or a little worrisome. Aunt Mamie taught me that a lady, a proper lady, was expected to wear a traveling hat.

We were on board the wagons; Ben and Tiger rode with Fred while I got to ride with Papa. As we turned onto the street where Fitch's Mercantile was located, we noticed a bunch of people milling about.

Fred pulled his wagon up by ours. "What's this?"

Papa took off his hat and scratched his head. "I don't rightly know."

Suddenly fifty people, maybe more, rushed toward us. I'd never seen such a crowd, not since our 'Turn of the Century' parade in Asheville.

"It's the Nashes!"

"We all came to say goodbye."

Papa said, "Looks like our leaving has stirred up a commotion."

"Goodbye, George, Ociee, Ben."

The gathering encircled us.

"Hello and goodbye again to you, Fred!"

"Good luck in your new home. The whole of Abbeville will visit you in Memphis!" laughed Mr. Fitch. "Only kidding, George."

Papa said, "Homer, you didn't let on to this when you dropped off your wagon."

"If I had, George, you'd gone the back way."

"You know me well, Homer."

Mrs. Adelaide handed Papa a basket of sandwiches. "We'll miss you, George, you and your charming children."

"Thank you, Adelaide." He passed the basket to me.

I was feeling shy in front of so many folks. I mumbled, "Real nice of you, Mrs. Adelaide."

"You're welcome, Ociee." She whispered, "You must never forget our bond. You and I are lady friends, as were Bertie and I."

I started to cry, didn't know if my tears were for sad or happy. I was just crying.

Mrs. Adelaide squeezed my hand. I held to hers tightly.

"Your mama is watching over her family, Ociee. You must never let go of that image. Bertie will walk beside you always."

"Yes, ma'am." I wiped my eyes.

Ben's schoolmates, Kelsey, Emma, Lucy, Alice, Willard and Stanley, were excused from their studies to say goodbye. My brother climbed down from his wagon and strutted around, totally full of himself. They asked him what he planned to do in Memphis.

"Don't know exactly. I'm either gonna become a riverboat captain or a conductor on a trolley car."

Ben's teacher, Miss Brown, standing to the side, appeared to be as upset as me. Ben suddenly raced over and gave her a hug. Miss Brown went to pieces. "You are an astounding boy, Ben Nash."

"Yes, ma'am. I know."

Miss Ethel, who owned the candy shop, handed me a

treat, a whole sack of penny candy, mostly butterscotch. "I know it's your favorite."

"Thank you, Miss Ethel. There couldn't be any candy as good as yours in all of Tennessee."

"Look there, children," said Papa, "Here comes Miss May."

We hurried to embrace the kind lady whose yummy baked goods were as sweet as her. Anytime we had need of comforting, Miss May always appeared with one of her cakes, cookies or fudge, honey buns or a fresh fruit pie. I should have told her about Fred having his own Mae, but I clean forgot.

Papa walked over and embraced Miss May.

"George Nash, you handsome devil," she squealed.

Ben and Fred cracked up. I didn't know what to think.

Papa winked at Miss May the same way he'd winked at me about the fiddle.

He looked around at each and every face in the crowd. I thought he might shed tears, but he didn't, not Papa.

"I can't tell you how much my family and I appreciate this gathering. You make me want to stay. You're good people, genuinely good people. We'll not be forgetting our friends in Abbeville."

Suddenly, Mrs. Hutchinson, Mae's mother, scurried through the crowd with a package for her daughter.

"Fred, dear, would you be so kind as to take this to my Rebecca?"

"Of course, ma'am," he said stepping down to greet his mother-in-law. "It's good to see you. How is Mr. Hutchinson feeling? I know he's been under the weather."

"Much better, dear. Still exhausted from our wedding. You do understand."

"Certainly. I hope you both will soon come for a visit."

"Maybe we will. We miss our darling daughter. Deary me, we miss you, too, Fred."

I giggled to myself. *Maybe*. Like her daughter, Mae's mother had a hard time making up her mind, too. I was glad she was acting friendly to Fred. We suspected the Hutchinsons were upset with him for taking their daughter to Memphis.

Mr. Watts was in front of the bank, playing his fiddle. Sounded like a march, I couldn't tell with all the noisy well wishing. I had noticed Papa put his in the wagon.

"Get back in your places," said Papa. "I'm afraid if we linger much longer, we'll be tempted to stay forever."

The group began to chant, "Stay. Stay. Stay!"

Suddenly, Tiger jumped down from Fred's wagon. Ben took off after him. "Tiger!"

I leapt from Papa's wagon.

Ben's school friends, even Miss Brown, along with others joined in the chase. Tiger raced down the street past Fitch's, the candy shop, and the post office. As he rounded the corner, a yellow dog broke through the crowd and ran barking at Tiger's heels. Up a tree scurried Ben's cat as the playful dog yelped and howled. Ben shinnied up the tree to the rescue.

"Tiger, you come HERE!"

The cat yowled and yowled. He seemed terrified.

Finally, grabbing Tiger by his tail, Ben captured him. The cat gripped Ben with his claws. He made the most gosh-awful pain-filled noise as Ben dropped down into the dirt.

"Ben, is he hurt?"

"No, Ociee, but he will be."

Ben must have been awfully mad with Tiger. I knew my brother was upset, but I'd never heard him threaten an animal, much less a pet he loved. I didn't know what would happen next.

"Everything all right, son?"

"Yes, Papa. Tiger isn't hurt; he's scared is all. There's something I got to do. Where's Mrs. Adelaide?"

"I'm here, Benjamin."

"You know what we talked about?"

"Yes, Benjamin. I hoped you'd change your mind."

"I reckon Tiger changed my mind for me, Mrs. Adelaide. Tiger doesn't want to go with us. He likes being in Abbeville. Here, Mrs. Adelaide, Tiger is yours. I thank you for giving him a home."

"Benjamin, I believe you've made the right decision. I promise you, I will take care of Tiger. He will have his saucer of fresh milk every afternoon."

"Yes ma'am. Bye, Tiger. Be a good cat."

Ben whipped around and ran to Fred's wagon. Tears streamed down his cheeks. The whole crowd applauded.

As much as Ben loved attention, he kept running. He climbed into Fred's wagon and hid his face. Fred hugged Ben close.

Papa handed me the reins and stood up in our wagon. Looking into the crowd, he said, "I'm mighty proud of my son." Turning to the second wagon, "Ben Nash, you are one fine boy."

Holding Ben, Fred nodded.

"Unless something else happens, I believe the Nashes are leaving. So for myself, for Ociee, for Ben and for Fred, I say farewell. Thank you for the finest send off a fellow and his family ever had."

Papa sat down and snapped the reins. Maud trotted down the street.

I turned and waved as children ran behind our wagons. Mrs. Adelaide, holding Tiger firmly in her grasp, held his paw making him wave. I'm not sure Ben saw, but I'd tell him later.

"Do you really think Ben should have given Tiger to Mrs. Adelaide?"

"Yes, Ociee, no doubt about it. I'm convinced something tragic would have happened to the cat. I meant it when I told him how proud I was. Giving away Tiger was a painful thing to do. He's a good boy, our Ben."

"Papa, Ben's a good boy, even when he's being bad."

"Right you are, Ociee, how right you are."

"Look at Maud, she's prancing. She assumes our send-off was for her!"

"Let her think so."

"What's Mr. Fitch's horse's name?"

"Mule."

"The horse is a mule?"

"No, he's a horse named 'Mule.'"

"My goodness, Papa, Ben finally got himself a mule, and it's taking him to Memphis!"

Chapter 6

We had a full day yet to go, and I was already dog-tired from leaving. I wasn't about to complain though. Watching Papa as we bumped along on the dusty dirt road, I could see he was in good spirits and stronger than ever. I wanted to be like him. George Nash was the biggest, smartest papa in Mississippi. In a day or two, he'd be the best man in Tennessee.

"You and Ben doing all right back there?"

"About as well as anybody riding with Ben," Fred said. "Does he ever stop talking?"

"Only when he's asleep," I shouted back.

Everyone laughed, but Ben.

We stopped for rest after the first few miles. I hurried to console Ben.

"I'm sorry about Tiger."

"Did what I had to."

He pushed me away. Usually, I'd have pushed him back. I didn't because he was hurting.

Papa finished watering Maud and called to Ben. They went for a walk. When they came back, I could see Ben had been crying. Papa was holding Ben's hand. I'd never seen the two of them holding one another's hands.

"Ben Nash is our hero of the day," said Papa, as if he were proclaiming the news to every person in Marshall County. "This young man has performed a purely unselfish act by sharing Tiger with Adelaide Fitch, a lady who desperately needed a cat to cherish."

Fred shook Ben's hand.

Not wanting to be pushed away for a second time, I tried something else to cheer up my brother.

"Ben, did you know the horse pulling y'all's wagon is Mule?"

"It's a horse!"

"Tell him, Papa. Tell him about Mule."

"Ociee is teasing you, Ben. You'll like this one, too, Fred. For some reason, Mr. Fitch decided to name his horse 'Mule.' Goodness only knows why, but it does provide us with a joke this morning."

I walked over to introduce myself to Mr. Fitch's horse.

"Mule, I'm Ociee Nash. Over there is my brother Ben. Are your ears still attached? I thought maybe he'd talked them off."

"Very funny." Ben came up to the horse. "This is my sister, Ociee. She's as stubborn as a *real* mule."

*

Soon after we passed through Waterford I spotted a sign which read, *Holly Springs, 10 miles*.

"Ten more miles, Papa! I'm about dead, and I'm covered in dust. Wish we could have taken the train."

"Ociee, we've been through this."

"I know, Papa." I remembered I wasn't going to complain.

"Whoa, Maud. These horses need food and water, and time to rest. I know we could use something to eat and drink ourselves. Ociee, spread this cloth over there in the pine grove while I tend to the horses. Fred and Ben, you can help with our meal."

"Yes, sir. My bottom sure is so sore!"

Fred left Ben with me and walked over toward Papa. He was talking to him about something, but I couldn't hear what he was saying. It didn't matter, I was too busy digging into the basket we brought from home and arranging Mrs. Adelaide's yummy sandwiches.

"Come and get it."

As we sat under the trees eating, I eyeballed Miss Ethel's

candy. Ben saw where I was looking. Quick as fire, we both lunged for the sack.

"Ociee, Ben, stop this minute! There are more than enough sweets for everyone here and an additional wagonload of children. You must finish your good food before you touch the candy."

"But Papa," argued Ben, "Candy IS good food."

"Ben, he means good FOR you food." Actually, I didn't care if the candy was good for us or not. I simply didn't want my brother to take more of his share of butterscotches.

Papa stretched out on the soft pinestraw. "Enough. Now listen to Fred. He has an announcement which may cheer us on, mostly you, Miss Ociee."

How right Papa was. Fred had arranged for us to stay overnight a mile north of Holly Springs. My brother had friends there, the Caldwells. Their son Jacob worked with him on the Illinois Central. Jacob's parents insisted Fred and the rest of us spend the night at their place. They could also provide a barn for the horses. Best of all, we'd be sleeping inside. What a relief.

According to the road signs, Papa figured we'd be there before dark. Thank glory, he was correct. When we arrived, five total strangers came running from the house shouting words of welcome. Their enthusiasm reminded me of our Abbeville farewell. The curious thing to me was we'd never met these people.

Papa tipped his hat, stepped down from the wagon, and tied up Maud.

"We're finally here, Mrs. Caldwell, it's been one long day," said Fred as he instructed Ben to tie up Mule.

"Come on, Ociee," encouraged Papa.

My shyness again washed over me. I wasn't comfortable with all their friendliness. I held out my arms for Papa's help. As he lifted me down, I asked him a question.

"Are these folks what you and Fred were whispering

about when we stopped?"

"Yes, you don't miss much, do you? I didn't want to get you all worked up about meeting family."

"Family?"

"Yes, Ociee, family."

"Mrs. Caldwell, Mr. Caldwell, thank you so much for sharing your home with us," said Papa as he held my hand and gestured toward Ben and Fred.

"These are mine and Bertie's children, Ociee here is the youngest. There's Ben. Fred, you know."

Right then, Papa could not have been very proud of Ben or me. Dumbstruck, we didn't move. Neither of us said the first word, not even a 'Hello.' The newfound relatives almost certainly took us for mutes.

As it turned out, the Caldwells, Dorothy and Samuel, were close friends of Mr. and Mrs. Archibald Wright and a widow named Annie Kate Milam. Even though they'd never met our mama or our papa, we were distantly related. Papa referred to them as *shirt-tail kin*, which, he explained, meant "only barely."

Papa said Southern people like to make connections. Also, because our mama was shirt-tail kin to Mrs. Milam, naturally, the Wrights would claim us, too. The three of them were already what they termed *close kin* with one another. Neither Ben nor I caught on or cared, but we were acting polite, smiling and listening, and trying to be eager like the grown people. Seemed to us the best way to behave.

*

Fred told Ben and me the story of how he found our shirt-tail relatives.

Fred said he was working a train run with Jacob Caldwell. Jacob invited him for Sunday dinner with his family during their stopover in Holly Springs. While they were eating, he was talking about Mama and mentioned she'd passed away three years back. Because of Mrs. Milam having the same name, he referred to Mama by her whole name, "Susan Alberta Milam Nash."

Mrs. Milam, who was Mrs. Caldwell's best friend, was frequently at their house for dinner, because she didn't cook. She sat straight in her seat and said, "Young man, your mother's name is Milam?"

"Yes ma'am, same as yours. Of course, it's her maiden name. Don't think Papa had it put on her tombstone."

"What a shame, such a fine name," she frowned. "We were meant to meet, young man! I'm certain we're related through your mother and my late husband. This is destiny!"

"Yes, ma'am." Fred didn't know what else to say.

He didn't need to say anything, because Mrs. Milam took charge. "Fred, you must gather us together."

Mrs. Caldwell agreed. "This is thrilling, we'll have the reunion here! The Wrights, Mrs. Milam, and the Nash family, us and Jacob, should he be available."

"How lovely, dear. Your home is perfect for entertaining."

"I'll bake my best rolls," offered Mrs. Wright.

Fred, who could be a little bashful like me, wondered what he'd gotten started. "I, I, I thank you."

Jacob came to his rescue. "Mother, Father, it's been grand to be home for dinner, but Fred and I really must leave. The train's whistle will be calling us any minute. I want enough time to kiss you goodbye, Mother."

"Jacob, I miss you already."

"Goodbye, Father."

"Take care, son."

"I will, sir."

"Again, your chicken was delicious, Mrs. Caldwell. Nice meeting you and Mr. Caldwell, and you, Mr. and Mrs. Wright. Mrs. Milam, so good to meet you."

"Destiny, Cousin Fred, destiny!"

Mrs. Caldwell made herself a note: *Prepare fried*

chicken for the Nashes.

As they made their way into Holly Springs, Jacob said, "You look a little pale, my friend. What's the trouble?"

"I don't quite know what to do about my new kinfolks. I'll talk with Papa next time we stop in Abbeville. Need his thoughts. We're not accustomed to having a big family."

The train's whistle blew. The young men hurried to the station.

Believing Mama would be pleased, both Fred and Papa adjusted to the idea of getting to know her shirt-tail kin. So when Papa was in Memphis, he and Fred had made plans. Fred wrote to the Caldwells, who happily contacted the Wrights and Mrs. Milam with an approximate date of arrival. Shortly before Fred left for Abbeville, he sent a telegram to the Caldwells.

Nashes coming STOP
Arrival Monday evening STOP
Thank you Fred STOP

Had Ben and I known the facts before we arrived at the Caldwell's, we may not have acted oddly. But then again, Papa was probably right, about me, in particular. I would have fretted about meeting those folks every bumpy mile of our trip.

Chapter 7

Mrs. Caldwell insisted we call her "Grannie Dot." She was so warm and welcoming, I quickly found my voice. Something about her reminded me of Aunt Mamie.

"Grannie 'Dot,' like a dot on our Mississippi map."

"Why yes, young lady. Remember where this *Dot* is located, in Holly Springs, Mississippi. You're always welcome here."

Mrs. Milam put her arm around me. "Now, Dot, remember, these are *our* newly discovered cousins, mine and the Wrights."

"Well, I suppose you're correct *technically*. Even so, I'm going to claim them. After all, Ociee, Ben and George are Fred's family, and he's part mine now because of our Jacob."

"Nonetheless, I'm Mrs. Milam, or to you, Annie Kate. I married into your late mother's family years and years ago. How I wish we'd known about you people sooner. Your mother must have been a charming woman. I assume so by getting to know Fred and now you sweet children."

"Yes, ma'am, err, Miz Annie Kate. Would you like to see her picture?"

"Yes, I would."

I rushed to the front bedroom where Ben and I were to sleep. I knew exactly where I'd put the painting. Miz Annie Kate followed closely behind.

"Here's Mama. Doesn't she have a beautiful smile?"

"Yes, she does. You favor her, Ociee, except for your blond hair."

"I keep praying for it to turn brown."

"I hope not! You're lovely exactly as you are."

First Fred had complimented my hair, now this brand new relative said she appreciated it, too. I was beginning to like my blond curls.

"Thank you, Miz Annie Kate." I carefully repacked Mama's picture.

Grannie Dot fried chicken for us, my favorite, Fred's, too. She also prepared sweet potatoes, greens, and black-eyed peas. For dessert, we had fresh churned strawberry ice cream.

Papa shifted in his chair. "This was a delicious meal, Dot. My children and I appreciate your hospitality."

"You're welcome, George."

After supper, the grown folks gathered in the parlor to talk. Ben and I were sent off to bed. I felt kind of funny kissing Papa goodnight in front of all those people, so, like a silly goose, I shook his hand and everyone else's. Even worse, by the time I got to Miz Annie Kate, I curtsied.

"Little cousin, I must give you a hug."

I hugged her back. I turned around and hugged Grannie Dot, too.

"Far superior to a handshake, isn't it?"

"Yes, 'um."

Papa blew me a kiss. "Angels on your pillow, sweet girl."

"Yours, too, Papa."

Being in a strange bed made it hard to sleep. I licked the last taste of Grannie Dot's strawberry ice cream from my upper lip.

"Milam Madstone," the words shook me wide awake. I prodded Ben. "Ben, listen!" My brother was sleeping like a dead tree.

I got up and crept to the door.

"I never put stock in tall tales," I heard Papa say.

"George, I tell you, it works," insisted Miz Annie Kate. "It's been in my husband's family since 1833. I, myself, am frequently called upon to bring the Madstone to the injured."

"How interesting," Papa yawned. He was exhausted but trying to be mannerly.

Miz Annie Kate continued, "The Madstone is the size of a small hen's egg with porous dents."

"Uh, hmmm."

I hoped my papa wouldn't doze off and fall out of his chair.

"People in Holly Springs, hundreds of them, have been cured by its touch. The stone has powers to treat snakebites, dog bites, bites from spiders, wounds from anything poisonous. It's most effective in treating rabies."

"Is that so?" replied Fred.

"Pretty remarkable," echoed our papa.

My ear to the bedroom door, I could hear fairly well. Papa seemed interested even if he was tired. As farmers, we knew about rabid animals. If a dog with rabies bites a person, it could kill him.

I remembered hearing about a Waterford man who died after being attacked by a rabid raccoon. We thought Fred was trying to scare us, but the story turned out to be true. He told us the man went completely mad, said he was foaming from his mouth just before he passed away.

I heard Fred ask how the Madstone works.

"First, I boil it in sweet milk. I place the warm stone directly on the person's injury. It suctions itself to the infected area and draws out the poison. The milk turns green."

Green milk. I gagged.

"The Madstone is applied over and over until the poison is gone. Afterwards, I soak the stone in water. My gracious, the smell is dreadful! Once it dries out, the Madstone is ready for treating the next patient."

I went back to bed and covered my head with a pillow. I didn't want to vomit all over Grannie Dot's company bed.

*

The next morning, I found Papa out in the Caldwell's barn. He'd slept there, saying he felt better staying close to our things.

"Papa, do you believe in the Madstone?"

"I don't think so. Wait a minute, how'd you know about it?"

"I was listening through the door."

"Doesn't surprise me."

"Papa, pretend you believe. Could we have used the Madstone on Mama's measles?"

Papa put down the water bucket.

"Ociee, I would have tried anything on this earth to save your mama. No, dear girl, the Madstone was no match for measles. Come over here and give your papa a good morning hug."

"I need one. I about threw up all Grannie Dot's good dinner when Miz Annie Kate started describing the green milk."

"Me, too. What do you say we load up and take our family to Memphis?"

"I'm ready."

"Maud, are you and Mule rested?"

Maud snorted. I took it for 'Yes.' Mule gave no reply

After another tasty meal we offered to clean up, but Grannie Dot replied, "No one cleans my kitchen to my standards."

Mr. Caldwell shook Papa's hand.

"Fine family, you have, George. Jacob thinks the world of your Fred. I believe both of our boys have the makings of first-rate railroad men."

"Couldn't agree with you more, Samuel. Say, didn't Fred tell me you were with the railroad yourself?"

"Yes, sir, but not like Jacob and Fred. I was a ticket man in Holly Springs for close to 20 years. These days, instead of listening for train whistles, I hear the songs of my cows mooing. It's far more peaceful."

Papa took off his hat, fanning himself. "There's nothing quite like the country."

I wondered if our papa would ever stop missing his farm.

*

We swapped places for our second day of travel. Papa took a turn with Ben and I got on board with Fred and Mule.

"Again, Dot, Samuel, thank you," said Papa with a wave. "My family couldn't have survived this journey without your help. Thanks also for your ongoing kindness toward Fred."

"Think nothing of it, George. Come again," replied Mrs. Caldwell. I knew she meant it. Sometimes people say things about visiting, but they don't really mean for folks to come.

It was gratifying how we'd made friends with the Wrights, the Caldwells, Grannie Dot, in particular. I was intrigued with Miz Annie Kate. I yearned to write about everyone in my journal, but with the jostling, I'd only make a scribbled mess. I'd trust my memory for the time being. Mama would appreciate us connecting with her family, even if we were barely related.

*

The sign read, *Byhalia, 10 miles*.

I groaned, "I've never ridden this far in a wagon without getting to where I was going."

Fred put his arm around me. "We'll be taking a rest in a couple of hours."

"Drat, Fred, we were rushing around so, I forgot to tell Ben about the Milam Madstone."

"What were you saying? Oh yes, while we were getting the horses ready, Papa mentioned you were all whipped up about the Madstone. It's a good thing you didn't bring it up to Ben. He'd still be asking questions."

"I expect you're right."

"Giddup, Mule. Ociee, you do realize we have a good

thirty miles to go?"

"You think we can do it, Fred?"

"We Nashes can do anything." He winked at me, same as Papa. I noticed a younger version of our papa's face atop my big brother's shoulders.

Papa suddenly pulled Maud to a halt.

Fred stopped Mule. "What the devil is going on?"

"Ben jumped down! He's heading toward the creek," shouted Papa. "The boy has no sense, no sense at all!"

I didn't fault Ben. I thought about joining him to wash up myself. I was sticky all over from sweat.

"Ben, get yourself out of there! Get out this minute."

"But I need my feet wet, Papa. They're hot."

"I'll get him, Papa, you and Ociee stay in the wagons."

Fred hurried down to the edge of the pond. Suddenly there was ripple in the grass. It moved again, revealing a copperhead snake.

Ben never saw it coming.

Chapter 8

"Look out, Ben!" Fred stepped in the water, boots and all, and grabbed Ben. He rescued his little brother, but not before the snake got its fangs into Fred's arm.

"Dear God."

Papa sprang for the wagon and bounded down the hill.

"Fred!"

"It got me, Papa. Ben's safe, but I'm in trouble."

Ben moaned. "I'm sorry, Fred. I didn't mean for this to happen. Please, Papa, will Fred be all right?"

Papa didn't answer. He dropped to his knees, opened his knife, and ripped Fred's sleeve. Holding my brother's arm, he began to suck out the venom.

I knew for certain Fred's arm was starting to swell. I stood helplessly, holding the two horses' reins and watching Papa from up on the rise. The situation was bad, really bad.

Dog bite. Poison. Snake bite. I had to do something. I tied Mule to a tree and pulled off Maud's harness. My traveling hat secure, I leapt on the horse's back. Kicking her harder than I intended, we galloped away. I prayed harder with every thunderous hoof beat.

"Please, Lord, don't let Fred die. Don't let Papa swallow any venom and die with him! Come on Maud, I know how fast you are! Go girl!"

Her feet pounded the road. Dust flew. Birds scattered. Squirrels scampered out of our way.

"Dear Lord, don't let me fall off."

All the angels above must have held me on Maud. She was running faster than the wind; I was stuck tighter than glue. My hat's brim was blowing straight backwards.

The sun was up. My heart was pounding. Tears streamed

from my eyes. How could such a bird-filled, blue-sky morning turn into this nightmare? All I knew was I believed in Miz Annie Kate Milam and in her Madstone.

"Come on, Maud!"

The horse panted.

Holly Springs, 2 miles. Thank glory, Fred thought we had come further.

Mama, are you here?

Papa used to say his Bertie must have been born on a horse, the way she could ride. Maybe I didn't have her pretty brown hair, but I surely could sit a horse. That day, staying on Maud was all that mattered. I had to get to Holly Springs. I had to find Miz Annie Kate's house.

"Mama, Mama, guide me." Her locket dangled from around my neck. I couldn't worry about losing it now. Fred mattered much more than my precious locket. "Mama, I believe you can see us from Heaven. Watch over your Fred. Please help Papa and ME!"

Holly Springs, 1 mile.

"Don't you fail me now, Maud. We're almost there."

Lavender. Mama is near.

"Ociee? Ociee Nash, is it you?" called a voice.

A buggy was heading my way.

"Maud, don't hit it!"

"Ociee, stop!" It was Grannie Dot.

I slowed Maud much as I could and screamed, "Fred got a snake bite! Where's Miz Annie Kate, her Madstone?"

"She's at my house! Quick, go left at the next turn. I'll fetch Doc Tom."

The Caldwell's house? The Madstone? I didn't know what to do, but I did it anyway. I turned left and galloped into the front yard. I tied Maud, and crashing up the steps, panting, I stumbled.

"Miz Annie Kate!"

"Yes."

"Do you have the Madstone?"

She opened a leather pouch. There it was, the Milam Madstone.

"Fred's snake bit. Please help!"

Miz Annie Kate rushed to the Caldwell's kitchen, poured warm milk into a pitcher, and hurried me to her buggy. Just then, Mr. Caldwell came around the side of the house.

"Samuel, please see to the Nash's horse. Fred's hurt, I've got Ociee. We'll explain later!"

I was grateful for Mr. Caldwell. I didn't have the first plan about caring for Maud.

"Giddy up, girl. Better hang on tight, Ociee, this won't be a leisurely ride. Try to steady the pitcher the best you can. The cure can't work without milk."

"Yes ma'am."

"We're going on the Byhalia road, correct?"

"Yes, they're a little over two miles away, down on the right by a pond." I held a death grip on the buggy's arm.

"Don't worry, I often drive fast in an emergency."

"I'm fine. Just worried about Fred is all." In truth, I'd never seen a lady drive like Miz Annie Kate. I was safer atop Maud!

Milk sloshed everywhere, over me, onto Miz Annie Kate, and in her buggy.

"Not to worry, dear, I poured more than an ample amount. You said your papa's tending to Fred?"

"Yes."

"Why didn't he send Ben for help, his being older and a boy."

"He didn't send me, Miz Annie Kate. I took off on my own."

"Lord, have mercy, child. You are one brave little girl."

"Yes, but Papa's gonna kill me."

"Not likely, Ociee. He'll be proud of you, once he sees our Madstone work its magic." She cracked the whip, her horse went all the faster.

"Oh Mama, oh Lord," I whispered, "please let us get there, and not TOO LATE."

I spotted the milepost we'd passed before Ben jumped. "We're almost there!"

Dust was flying everywhere. Dust and milk! We came to the top of a small rise. "There they are, I see Papa!"

"Papa!" I leapt from the buggy. It's a wonder I didn't spill what remained of the milk.

Running down the hill, I was hollering, "We got it, we got the Madstone!"

Papa stood, his arms in the air. "Where in the devil have you been, Ociee?"

He was mad as a bull. I could see it in his eyes, but I didn't care.

"Where's Fred? Is he all right?"

"No, he's not all right. We need to get your brother to a doctor, and fast! No thanks to you, I didn't dare leave. I was about to send Ben to look for you, Ociee Nash. Dag nabit!"

Papa had never been as angry with me, not in my whole life.

Miz Annie Kate, holding her long black skirt, waved her hand and pointed to the bag with the Madstone

"George Nash, move out of my way!"

"Yes ma'am."

She dropped down beside my brother. "How are you, Fred?"

"Been better, Miz Annie Kate. Papa tried to suck out the venom."

Miz Annie Kate opened the pouch and dropped the stone in the milk. She applied it to Fred's arm, securing it with a white rag.

"What's THAT?" Fred asked.

"It's the Milam Madstone. You remember, I told you

about it last night. Never dreamed we'd need it for you!"

In fear and disbelief, Fred stared at the rock, which, by then, was stuck firmly to his arm.

"Calm yourself, Fred. It'll begin working quickly."

I watched her every move. Actually, seeing Miz Annie Kate use the Madstone was far more interesting than listening to her though the door. For some reason, *watching* didn't turn my stomach upside down the way *hearing* had. Fred made the difference. A sister can't be sensitive when her brother needs her.

"The dern thing is sucking on my arm!"

"Good! The Madstone is working. Now, Fred, lay back and breathe deeply. As long as the stone creates suction, it's drawing out venom."

I breathed deeply along with Fred. I also thanked Mama and the good Lord.

Out of the corner of my eye, I saw Papa talking to Ben. My brother felt responsible for the snakebite. He was carrying on as if he was injured. In truth, he was. Ben's spirit was shattered.

Everyone's panic began to settle. I snuggled up to Fred and held his hand while the stone finished its job. Miz Annie Kate sat next to me, and together we watched over him. Papa and Ben stood close by. Still not himself, Fred remained weak. Mercifully, the swelling was going down; Papa and Miz Annie Kate were assured he'd recover.

"George, your rapid response made a big difference. Fred's young and strong; he'll get along perfectly well. A copperhead, was it?"

"Not sure," muttered our brother. "It looked like one; red with brown coloring. Scared the fool out of me."

Papa nodded *Yes*.

Fred forced himself to continue. "Had to stop it, the dern thing was after Ben. Couldn't believe it bit me."

"Shhhhh, rest, son."

Carefully, because I didn't want to dislodge the stone, I patted Fred's strong shoulder. "Thank glory for you, Fred. You saved Ben."

"He's worth it. Sometimes."

Ben said nothing in reply. He couldn't. He stood by himself over by a pine tree trying to figure out how to act, what to do.

I, on the other hand, grinned at Fred's welcomed tease. It meant he was better.

"Our Ben is worth saving," I insisted. Still, no response came from Ben. We understood to leave him be.

"I'll say it again," I continued, "Thank glory for Fred. And for Papa, and for Mrs. Miz Annie Kate and her Madstone."

"As long as we're being thankful, Ociee Nash," said Miz Annie Kate, "let's be thankful for you."

"I did ride mighty fast and without falling off. Didn't even have a bridle. So thank glory for ME," I bragged, "And for Maud, too. Our horse has never galloped that fast. Maud wanted to save Fred."

I didn't want to let on too much, but I was mighty pleased with me.

Fred sat up and propped against a tree. "Ociee, wait a minute. What happened? Where'd you go? All I recall was Papa going crazy when you took off."

"I went to get the Milam Madstone."

Fred looked at his arm. "So I see. But how'd you find Miz Annie Kate?"

Before I could answer Fred, Papa put his hands on my shoulders. "Whoa, hold on a minute, Ociee. Where IS Maud?"

I was itching to tell the whole story, but first I had to ease Papa's mind.

"Mr. Caldwell is seeing to her."

I explained about coming up on Grannie Dot and how

she told me Miz Annie Kate was already at the Caldwell's house with the Madstone.

"Miz Annie Kate came by to show it to us. Grannie Dot left her to find us. She figured her buggy could go fast enough to catch our wagons. Grannie Dot planned to talk Papa into turning around."

Papa listened, shaking his head with every word.

"Ociee, you scare me, but you amaze me, too. I'd wouldn't have dreamed you'd know your way to Holly Springs, much less to the Caldwell's."

"I pay attention."

"Ociee, I was extremely worried about you. But my concern aside, you succeeded in helping Fred. I'm grateful and mighty proud."

"Thank you, Papa." I was so thrilled to earn his praise, I almost cried.

In front of everybody, he added, "Ociee Nash, it's plain to see you're smart, and brave, and a fine horsewoman. I should not have gotten so angry. Please, will you forgive me?"

"Yes, Papa." Then I did cry. I hugged tight to him and whispered in his ear, "I knew it'd blow over once Fred was fixed."

"You are one special girl."

"I know."

"Ociee, you sound like Ben," said Fred. My big brother was back to acting himself.

"Annie Kate," said Papa, "You were at the Caldwell's?"

"Yes, how was I to know you people would be leaving at the break of dawn? I was certain to find you there. Because we'd talked about the Madstone last night, I wanted to show it to Fred and the children. Little did I dream its powers would be called upon today!"

I thought to myself, *But Mama knew*.

"I can't wait to see Mae's face when she hears about

this."

Papa said, "Your bride is going to skin me alive."

"Can you blame her?" laughed Fred. "Ociee, my Mae will be astonished by what you did."

"She will?" I really wanted him to repeat what he said!

Miz Annie Kate cleared her throat. "Ahem, Cousin Ociee, do we have the Nash men believing in our Madstone?"

Papa answered for me. "Safe to say, I'm convinced. Wouldn't you agree, Fred?"

"I'm living proof. Annie Kate, do you think we're finished?"

"Almost," she replied. "Try to be patient, Fred. "Won't be long now."

Everyone was resting. Ben glanced briefly at the Madstone. Walking slowly to the top of the hill, he gave Mule a drink of water from the pond. My brother stroked the horse's mane, consoling himself about Fred in the only way he understood. Ben was always comfortable with animals.

Fred had drifted to sleep on our mama's quilt, one I'd brought him from our wagon. Miz Annie Kate and Papa talked quietly in the shade of a nearby tree. They kept their eyes on Fred and on Ben, too.

I sat in a clump of weeds frantically lacing a daisy chain. Like my churning insides, the chain turned into a knotted mess. I closed my eyes and tried to relax as I listened to the serene chirping of a sweet mother bird. Nothing. I could not will myself to feel peaceful.

I went to Ben. "Are you feeling better?"

"Reckon I will, some day. Maybe. Ociee, if Fred had died, it would have been my fault!"

Tears washed Ben's face. I didn't know what to say. I tried to hug him, but as usual, he didn't accept my attention.

A white wagon pulled up. Down the slope came Grannie

Dot with a stranger.

"Sorry we took so long," she said trying to catch her breath. This is . . . "

"I'm Doc Tom."

"Doctor, I'm George Nash. Thank you for coming."

"You're welcome. You folks look more like you're having a picnic than a tending a snakebite."

"Thankfully, the worst of this seems to be over."

"I'd still like to take a look, if I might."

"Please, we've be grateful. My son Fred is right over here."

Papa spoke with Grannie Dot while Doc Tom checked Fred's arm. "You never planned on us being such a bother. I'm truly sorry."

"George, we're practically family. I'm just relieved this incident turned out as well as it did. Won't you consider coming back to Holly Springs for the night? You folks ALL need to recover."

"Well, Dot, if you don't mind."

"George, I wouldn't have invited you, if we didn't want you to come. We have plenty of food left from last night. Besides, when Samuel hears what happened, he'd be furious were I not to return with you."

Papa's anguish melted away. He questioned Doc Tom about Fred's condition.

"Your son is doing fine, but he could use a good night's sleep."

"It's already arranged. Again, thank you, Doc, for coming to see about Fred."

"You're welcome. I hear you folks are on your way to Memphis, seems there's a certain young wife who's anxious to see Fred."

"Yes, but we'll not leave until he's up to traveling."

"He should be ready by morning."

As soon as Miz Annie Kate was in earshot, the doctor

said, "I declare, one of these days, that Madstone may put me out of business."

Miz Annie Kate replied, "Why, Doc Tom, I don't tend to more than eight or ten of your patients each month. You can't be serious."

"No, ma'am, I suspect there will always be a need for a doctor in Holly Springs. There ARE some things your magic rock cannot do!"

"A great many things, Doc Tom."

"I know what matters most to you and to me are our patients. We strive for everyone to be healthy."

"Amen, Doc Tom."

"Will there be any riders for my wagon?"

Papa nodded. "My son, Fred. Thank you."

My brother didn't argue.

*

Grannie Dot was one smart lady. She even thought to bring along an extra wagon horse from the Holly Springs livery stable. The horse was tied to the back of Doc Tom's medical wagon.

"Thank you, Dot."

"You are more than welcome, George. Now let's get on our way. My Samuel must be anxious. I left in quite a flurry this morning."

"Poor fellow. I can only imagine." Papa untied the livery horse and led him to our wagon.

Fred steadied himself and walked toward Ben. Like Papa so often did, he ruffled Ben's hair. "I want you to forget everything about this accident, because that's exactly what it was, an accident."

"Fred," Ben welled up again. "Fred, I'm sooo sorry. I didn't . . ."

"You're not *forgetting* it. Ben, what did I say?"

"You told me to forget it."

"Correct. Benjamin Nash, don't go wading anywhere

there is the slightest possibility of meeting up with a copperhead or with a snake of any kind. Do you hear me?"

"Yes."

Papa picked up the harness I'd tossed to the ground. "Ben, make yourself useful and gear up this horse."

"Yes, sir."

Papa swallowed hard. "Son, how would you feel about driving to Holly Springs? Think you could handle it?"

"Do *you* think I can, Papa?"

"I know you can, Ben."

"I'll do my best."

"All right then, Ociee and I'll drive this livery horse, just in case he's the nervous kind. You follow with Mule."

"Don't worry, Papa, I'll be watching out for you."

Papa's trust breathed Ben's spirit back into him.

Fred called back to Ben from Doc Tom's wagon, "Mississippi farm boy, you look mighty fine driving that wagon."

"Fred, I'm not a farm boy for long. I'm driving this wagon back to town, then I'm gonna go to Memphis to operate one of those trolley cars."

"Saints above, watch out, Memphis, here comes Ben Nash!"

Chapter 9

We'd been back at Grannie Dot and Samuel Caldwell's place for a couple of hours when Fred received a telegram from Memphis.

Snake bite STOP
Hurry home STOP
Be cautious STOP
Love to all
Mae STOP

"How in blue blazes did Mae find out?" Fred seemed more upset about Mae than he'd been about the copperhead.

"I'm afraid you have me to blame, young man," said Grannie Dot. "I knew the snake incident would set you back, so lest she worry, while the livery man was tying the horse to Doc Tom's wagon, I went across the street and wired your wife."

"Sorry, I don't mean to sound ungrateful. I just wish you'd not told her. Mae worries about me anyway, so hearing this likely sent her through the roof. "

"I understand, Fred. But do keep in mind it's always better for your marriage if your are totally honest with one another."

Mr. Caldwell raised both eyebrows and nodded.

"Yes, ma'am. I suppose you're right. But I was thinking Mae might take it better if she saw I was none the worse before she found out something happened."

Her husband shook his head mightily as if to say, "Hush up, boy."

Grannie Dot added, "I'd like to share another piece of

advice about women, your woman, in particular. From what you and Jacob have told me about her, Mae is quite intuitive. Could be she already sensed something was wrong. As time passed, she'd become frantic imaging all manner of tragedy: illness, accident, a fallen horse, robbers along the way. Shall I go on? Were you not supposed to arrive home before dark tonight?"

Grannie Dot didn't give Fred pause to answer.

"No, dear, Mae needed to know exactly what occurred. Your bride would lose trust were you to keep this from her. Even though your heart was in the right place, Fred, trying to shield her is not treating her with respect. Mae is a married woman capable of handling this."

About the only thing my brother could say was, "Yes, Grannie Dot." He sent Mae a telegram.

Husband fine STOP
Home tomorrow STOP
Everyone for supper STOP
Love from Fred STOP

I was comfortable and happy in Holly Springs and thrilled to have more time there. We would also get to eat another delicious meal at the Caldwells with Miz Annie Kate.

The other shirt-tail kin, the Wrights, had a church meeting and weren't able to be with us. Papa said he believed they were afraid to be around the Nashes because our luck might rub off. I hoped he was wrong. I didn't want to think my family could pass on bad fortune.

There was no doubt we'd leave the next morning; according to Papa, before the sun came up. He held to his promise. Before the Caldwell's rooster crowed, we were up bustling around like a bed of Abbeville ants.

"Fred's recovered," said Grannie Dot, "Look at him,

he's chomping at the bit."

She was right, my brother was moving faster than anybody besides Papa. Ben and I were dragging our feet. We dreaded the thirty-five-mile trip.

"Say goodbye, Ociee, Ben. Time's a wasting!"

Grannie Dot wiped away tears, "Don't know how I grew so attached to you folks in this short time."

Mr. Caldwell's husband consoled her. "Not to worry, my dear. I have a feeling we haven't seen the last of the Nashes."

I wondered about Mr. Caldwell's words. I didn't know if his 'feeling' was full of fear or meant in a positive way.

"I promise we'll come again!" I said, tossing my traveling bag in the wagon.

"Good girl, Ociee," said Grannie Dot giving me a kiss on my cheek.

"Me, too," echoed Ben jumping off their front porch and bounding over the fence.

Papa scowled, "If we return, we'll try not to bring trouble."

"How can you make such a promise, Papa?" asked Fred. "You couldn't possibly leave Ben at home!"

He got a big laugh from everyone but Ben.

"Quit picking on me." He screwed up his face. Truth was, Ben liked Fred's teasing, because it meant things were back to normal.

Once again we said our goodbyes; once again I felt the loss down in the hollow of my stomach. I wished every person I knew could live in the same place. I hoped I could keep my promise to Grannie Dot about returning to Holly Springs. For me, disappointing Aunt Mamie by not going back to North Carolina had been bad enough.

We hadn't gone a mile down the road when Ben started harping at Fred to turn over the reins.

"Come on, Fred. Please, you need to relax."

"Relax? How could I with YOU driving?"

"I did a great job yesterday. Papa said so."

"Hush up, Ben. Quit asking or I'll never do it."

Another grunt.

Papa chuckled. "Lots easier to listen to your brother riding behind us than when he's in the same wagon. By the time we stop for lunch, Fred may be looking for another snake to put him out of his misery."

"Papa, you don't mean it?"

"Come on, Maud, giddy up."

*

Going north toward Byhalia, we passed field after field of dirt rows striped with early springtime, those soon to be dotted green, cotton-white, and corn-gold. Shade trees and the occasional farm building scattered themselves in the patchwork landscape.

"Papa, is there any place in the world prettier than Marshall County?"

"Not many, Ociee girl."

I gazed first to the right, then left, then right again as Papa pointed out the hardwoods, oak trees, hickories, and chestnuts. To make sure they'd notice, I hollered back to Ben and Fred. Didn't want my brothers to miss a single sight.

"Is Memphis green, Papa? If I don't see trees I may lose my joy."

"Yes, Memphis has beautiful trees, flowers, bushes. You'll have all the green you need. We have several big trees in our yard. But, Ociee, you'll find your type of joy any place you are. It's your core spirit. Don't you remember a frightened nine-year-old who didn't want to go to Asheville?"

"Yes, I do. But then how I loved those Blue Ridge Mountains."

"I know you did. You'll find things to love in Tennessee,

too."

We rode by farms many times bigger than our old place; farms with cotton gins and gristmills. We also passed the ruins of churches and businesses, homes and barns, and deserted communities that seemed to cry out for people to return. As he often did, Papa grieved about the Civil War and how its devastation set back our part of the country.

"War is a terrible thing. People hurt, people dying, families destroyed. I don't know how long it'll be before folks get over this destruction and heartache. Thank glory, it's over."

"Could there be another war, Papa?"

"I pray not. Thankfully, most folks are tired of fighting."

"Hope so."

"You know, Ociee, you can promote peace."

"Me? I'm only eleven."

"When you treat folks kindly, they'll often respond in a positive way. A caring, sensitive person like you can serve as an example for others. Ociee, by holding to your beliefs about what's considerate, what's right, you'll be doing everything you can to promote peace."

My papa was the wisest man I ever knew.

*

"Wake up, Ociee, we're in Byhalia."

Goodness knows how I didn't tumble off the wagon. Half asleep, half awake, I replied, "Hoorah, my bottom's not even sore."

Papa laughed. I was embarrassed. It was the truth, but I didn't mean to say such a thing out loud.

I was thankful we stopped, because it gave me more time in Mississippi. Before we left Abbeville, I'd studied a big wall map at Fitch's. Tennessee looked like a long skinny anvil with Mississippi holding it up. Maybe Tennessee sat atop Mississippi? Could it squash us; might it squash me?

Fred took Mule and Maud to drink from a farmer's pond

while I put out Grannie Dot's picnic lunch. I missed her already.

"Any snakes?" yelled Ben.

"If I spot one, I'll call you!"

"Be careful, Fred," I warned. "We're traveled too far from Miz Annie Kate's Madstone."

"We should make it to Memphis by suppertime," announced Papa.

"Halleluiah!" cheered Fred.

My heart sank. "Ben, are you excited?"

"Sure am."

Everyone was glad but me. I comforted myself biting on a cold fried chicken leg. I'd work on my joy later.

"It's mighty nice of Mae to have supper for us," Papa told Fred. "Your wife is a thoughtful young woman. I hope we won't be troubling her for long."

"Papa, I can ease your mind."

Fred started acting like Ben *and* me. We had trouble keeping secrets. Now our full-grown brother was grinning big as a fool about something, a secret, I reckoned.

"Supper will be waiting for us in YOUR house on East Pontotoc."

"How can that be, son?"

"We wanted to give you a warm Memphis welcome and make you feel at home. Last week, Mae and I and some friends got your house ready, cleaned, hung curtains, laid in supplies. All we'll have to do is empty these wagons, and I've arranged for help with that."

"You're one good man, Fred Nash. We thank you."

"I'm your son. Enough said." Fred turned to me. "Now, Ociee, once we unload, you'll pick the best spots for Mama's quilts, her vases, and such."

"I'll try."

"You can do it," said Papa. "You made perfect our home in Abbeville."

He lifted my chin to his face. Then looking wistfully at Mama's locket, Papa took it in his big left hand. Framed by his fingers, the locket appeared so tiny and delicate.

"I'm asking you to bring your mama inside our new home, Ociee. You're the lady of the house now."

"I am?"

My mind was awhirl. I was honored to be the lady of the house, and real pleased to be in charge of decorating. At the same time, I was a tad overwhelmed. Perhaps it was because I would be sleeping in three different places in four nights, four, counting my nap in the wagon. First, I'd been in my bed in Abbeville, and then we spent two nights in Holly Springs, next we'd be sleeping in another house. I would have to rely on other times when I had to deal with change.

Aunt Mamie would term what I needed *adaptability.*

"Ociee, it's rather simple," she'd say. "You must engage your positive spirit and adapt to new circumstances."

Papa, my brothers and I sat under a hickory tree. The soothing breeze blew as we ate our last meal in Mississippi.

I'd adapt.

I'd be positive.

My worries gave in slowly but surely to my hopes.

Chapter 10

"The Frisco Railroad has opened up this old town," said Fred as he finished his cookie. "It's a marvelous thing for the folks around here."

"Let's hope you're right, son. In my way of thinking, the South's recovery is taking far too long."

"Fred, I'm real proud you're a railroad man," I said.

Ben reached for an apple. "Reckon I could be one some day?"

"There's no shortage of ideas from you, Ben," said Papa. "Nashes, I wish our meal could go on forever, but we'd better get on our way. We still have 20 miles to Mae's cooking."

We rinsed our dishes in the pond with no sight of a snake. I wrapped up what was left in case anyone was hungry before we got home. Home. The horses ready, we prepared to depart. Papa had Ben with him. It was my turn with Fred.

"Do you really think I'll be good at decorating?"

"I do, Ociee. Don't forget what Papa said. You're the lady of the house."

I giggled, "Makes me feel like a sure enough grown person."

"You almost are grown, and only eleven years old." Fred got serious. "Ociee, it fills me with sadness to realize how fast you had to grow up. I was seventeen when Mama died, much older than you and Ben. And we had Papa, of course, but you were the only girl. I always worried about you. Eight years old and there you were, left hanging out like a lone bed sheet on the clothesline. I know that's why Papa sent you to Asheville.

"I was fine."

"I know, but—" he began.

"But nothing, Fred Nash!" I stopped him. I was practicing my *adaptability* and my *joyful spirit*. "I love Aunt Mamie and Mr. Lynch, too. I met all sorts of nice folks there and played with children from my school, liked most of them, too. *Most*, but not the bad ones who caused Miss Small misery. I love Elizabeth and her parents. She's an *only* girl like me. You remember hearing about her, don't you, Fred?"

"I surely do know about Elizabeth and your 'Turn of the Century' parade. And how could I forget the Murphy's fire?"

"Their house and most of the contents burned up. It was awful. The fire started close to midnight, Aunt Mamie and I ran down Charlotte Street in our nightclothes. Everybody in the neighborhood came, but even the bucket brigade couldn't save the house. Afterwards, every person in town pitched in to help the Murphys."

"A tragedy brings out the best in folks."

"You sound like Papa!"

"So I hear."

"Elizabeth and her mother went to stay with relatives in Georgia. I missed them like I missed y'all, but I stayed extra busy. I had to help Mr. Murphy watch over his workers every day. He and I made sure Elizabeth's house was built back fast as possible."

Fred laughed, "I can only imagine."

"I was 'as patient as time allowed.' Aunt Mamie said so. She insisted the Murphys would never have gotten back into their home as quickly without my expert pestering."

"I'm sure she knew exactly what she was talking about."

I kept on babbling. I babbled whenever I got nervous.

"You'll not have to worry about me, Fred. I'll make friends in Memphis. I had hundreds in Asheville, neighborhood children along with interesting folks like Lavonia and Opal, Aunt Mamie's seamstress helpers, and Mr. Hightower, who ran the post office."

"I declare, Ociee, you talk as much as Ben!"

"Is it a bad thing?"

"No, not necessarily. I like to hear you being optimistic."

"*Optimistic* is as important as being brave."

"I suspect it is."

We were passing through Olive Branch when I noticed the railroad station.

"Look over there. Does your train make a stop in Olive Branch?"

Before he could say yes or no I told him I'd had seen buildings similar to the Olive Branch station. I figured I sounded optimistic and brave, AND well traveled.

Fred nodded yes. He had the identical expression on his face as Papa did when he was amused with me.

Memphis was getting closer with every passing hour. We stopped to rest, but promptly returned to the road. Ben asked to ride with Fred again because Papa wouldn't let him take the reins. He must have figured he'd have a better chance with Fred. Papa said no.

"Keep things as they are. Fred has something to discuss with Ociee."

Ben was too excited to argue.

I couldn't imagine what Fred had on his mind. But because I'd done most of the talking since lunch, he deserved a turn.

"Ociee, you've missed a whole month of school."

"I've tried to keep up with my work."

"I'm not surprised, you're a smart girl. Papa and I know how important school is to you. Now, Ben; he's another story. In fact, I've arranged for him to work with a tutor. But, Ociee, because you're better prepared, we've made other plans for you."

I sat up extra straight glowing like a Christmas star. First, I was optimistic; next, I was prepared. I batted my eyelashes and sashayed my shoulders.

"I told Papa, Mae and I found the perfect place, a school for girls."

"Just girls? What sort of school is that?"

I thought for a second. I was still mad at the dreadful boy who'd dipped my pretty pigtails in his inkwell. There would be no more shenanigans of that sort in a girls' only school.

Fred talked to me about St. Agnes Academy. Even the school's name was strange. Fred explained an academy is where smart people go to get smarter. I loved hearing the smart part.

"Agnes is a real pretty name, Fred, but I don't understand the 'saint' part."

"The school is named for a real holy person named Saint Agnes."

Smart and holy, both appealed to me. Fred then referred to the teachers at St. Agnes as "sisters."

"The teachers are all sisters? They must come from one huge family to be able provide enough women to run an entire school."

"Ociee, please just listen to me."

"I'll try."

One peculiar thing my brother told me about the sisters was everyone dresses exactly alike.

"Are some of them twins like Lavonia and Opal? They're the only girls I know who dress to match."

"No, first of all, the sisters are not related. They've chosen to join a group of women who strive to become closer to God. Dressing in the exact same outfit is part of vows they make when they become nuns."

"Nones?"

"Nuns. N-u-n-s is another word for sisters."

"So nuns are more concerned about students than about what they wear?"

"Yes."

Fred had learned a great deal about these ladies, the nuns or sisters, as I would call them. They were kind and smart, holy and heroic. They had cared for the War's wounded, even for Yankee soldiers, who came to Memphis to fight against Southerners. I could hardly believe my ears. They were people of peace, like Papa and me.

"Ociee, we know all too well, Mama died when the measles epidemic spread through Marshall County in 1897."

I bowed my head.

Fred stroked my hair as he told me Memphis experienced epidemics every bit as devastating as our measles.

"Yellow fever hit in 1867, 1873, and again in 1878. It was a fearsome disease that took the lives of countless good folks like our mama. It killed thousands and thousands, including more than 5000 people in 1878 alone."

I must have turned white because Fred added, "Don't be concerned, Ociee, yellow fever is long gone. The last epidemic was over before you were born."

He didn't go into much detail, but said he wanted me to learn important facts about the Sisters of St. Dominic.

"The brave sisters nursed persons stricken with the fever. Many, many of the nuns died along with their patients."

"What happened to the dead people's children?"

"The sisters took take care of the orphans. To this day, they continue to take in children in a place called St. Peter's Orphanage."

"St. Peter, the St. Peter we learned about in Sunday School?"

"The same."

"Am I an orphan?"

"Ociee, how could you be an orphan?" Fred kissed my forehead. "An orphan has no family. You have Papa and me and Ben."

"And Mae, and Aunt Mamie, and now Miz Annie Kate. And, if we're not counting real kin, Grannie Dot."

"You have the idea."

"And, the sisters, the Sisters of who?"

"St. Dominic."

"Is he a friend of St. Peter and St. Agnes?"

"I'm sure he is."

I figured out three things. First, there was something as horrible as measles. It's called yellow fever. Second, sisters are brave because they aren't afraid of epidemics. Third, I learned the sisters care about children called orphans, and about children like me, who have families. St. Agnes sounded like a wonderful place. I was going to like the school. Blood relatives, shirt-tail kin, or holy ladies; it was nice to realize all sorts of people choose to help young folks.

"Ociee, we're riding on Lamar Avenue," said Fred. "We're getting close."

"It's such a big street. Fred, cobblestones! Asheville has cobblestones, too. You don't think they'll injure Maud's or Mule's hooves, do you?"

Some horses are accustomed to pulling a buggy on stone and brick, as well as on dusty dirt, but ours were country horses.

"'Course not."

I could hear Ben screaming, "Go slower, Papa. I got to see!"

Ben Nash was so excited, it was a wonder he didn't fall off the wagon and get run over. He hadn't traveled to North Carolina like me, so Memphis was the first big town he ever saw. Looking around, however, I was starting to understand it was the biggest town I'd ever seen, too.

"Everybody," shouted Ben. "Look what's coming!"

"Ben, that's a horseless carriage," I hollered back to him. "Isn't it the grandest thing!"

My brother's jaw dropped.

Papa and Fred slowed the wagons. I was glad, because I needed to brag and wanted everybody to hear me.

"My friend Elizabeth's father up and bought one! Mr. Murphy calls it his 'motorcar.'"

"Elizabeth gets to RIDE in it?"

"Not yet. Mrs. Murphy is too fearful. She won't touch the motorcar herself and doesn't permit Elizabeth to get any closer than 25 feet."

The horseless carriage smoked and sputtered as it passed by. We couldn't talk loud enough to get above the racket. Fred and Papa held tight Maud and Mule's reins to keep them from bolting.

To our delight, the passenger waved to us. I returned the wave with both hands as Ben whooped and whistled. Because of all the smoke, I couldn't tell if the person was a man or a lady. *She* appeared to be wearing a skirt and a floppy hat. Peering out through a wide mask, the passenger looked exactly like a gigantic bumblebee.

The motorcar turned the corner.

"Ben, one of these days, you and I will have us a ride."

"Sure we will!"

"ALL of us," replied Fred as he wiped his face with a handkerchief. "Don't you be leaving out Papa, Mae, or me."

There was so much activity and so many people. What I was seeing was Abbeville but a hundred times larger. I saw more and more buildings as stores and houses popped up everywhere. People hurried about like ants after we poured well water into their hill. Children chased dogs; ladies hung out laundry; horse-drawn wagons came toward us, crossed in front of us, and passed as we marveled at the sights.

"Where's Main Street, Madison Avenue?" Papa asked. "Surely with all this commotion we're downtown."

"Not anywhere near," replied Fred. "Those streets are

closer to the river, and we're a good ways from there."

Fred, with Papa following close behind, turned Maud right onto East Street. We went left onto Linden.

"Ready, Ociee Nash? Ready to see your home?"

I couldn't swallow.

He clicked his tongue. As we turned up East Pontotoc Avenue, I saw a girl running from a house. It was Mae. She was waving and flapping her apron so much, I thought she might be carried up in the air.

"Fred, you Nashes, come to me!"

"We're finally here, Mae!"

Without waiting for Papa or Fred to stop, Ben and I jumped down from the wagons.

Mae ran toward us on a stone walk as she pointed to a beautiful white house, one with a friendly front porch and flowers blooming. A hickory tree, like the one under which we'd eaten lunch, shaded our home. There was a huge magnolia, perfect for climbing. Thank glory, Papa was right; we had green a plenty. I wanted to hug Mae. I wanted to rush inside. What I did was spin in circles shouting, "We're home. We're together FOREVER!"

Papa hitched the horses with Ben's help while I danced around the yard. It didn't bother me my face was filthy with road dirt or my hair was a frizzy mess from the wind and heat.

"Tell me about the copperhead snake, dear," said Mae as she tenderly touched Fred's arm.

"Can't I wait until after we eat?" said Fred, trying to pull his sleeve down so she wouldn't look at the bandage. "We're starving."

Fred took Mae's hand in his and walked up on to the porch. He gestured to me, to Papa and Ben. "Come on inside, Nashes. We want you to tell us what you think."

Ben bounded up the steps. He tugged at Mae's skirt. "I didn't bring Tiger."

"My poor Ben. What happened to your kitty?"

"Tiger's fine, happy as he can be. Mae, did you know cats don't like crowds or traveling or even water? He'd hate the Mississippi. I'm a hero. Papa said so. I gave my cat to Mrs. Adelaide because I'm not selfish."

"Good for you, Benjamin."

"Mrs. Adelaide calls me Benjamin!"

Papa was close behind Ben, but I stayed back. As I reached down to pick a daffodil, I couldn't help but overhear Mae.

She pushed back Fred's bandage. "Looks pretty angry."

"It's really nothing, Mae, a little nip. Let's talk about something else. Your mother sent you a package."

"Nice of her, but don't be changing the subject, dear husband. Little nip? What am I to do with you, Fred Nash?"

"You can quit worrying about me. To tell you the honest truth, Mae, it was worth getting the snakebite. You'll understand once you hear our story. Get Ociee to tell you about the Milam Madstone during dinner."

"About the *what*?"

Chapter 11

"Mae, thank you kindly. This was the finest supper I've had in years!"

"Thank you, Papa Nash," she replied. "I can only cook a few things, but I like to believe I do them well."

Fred was grinning like a contented cow. Fact was, our brother was so glad to be home with his bride, he would have been pleased to eat an old shoe.

"I married myself the best wife in all of Marshall County."

I was glad Fred didn't say "the prettiest girl in Marshall County," because Papa had given Mama that title. I reckon my brother remembered.

"My wife shouldn't be washing dishes. Stand aside, Mae, I'll take over."

"Thank you, dear. I want to help your family with a few things before we leave. Ben, your papa can show you to your room. It's right behind his."

Papa eyed Ben. "So I can keep my ears open should you take a mind to crawl out a window."

"I wouldn't do such a thing!"

"No, of course not, son. Not until you figure out some place interesting to go. You do recall sneaking out, or trying to, you and Stanley, just before the wedding?"

"Stanley isn't in Memphis, Papa."

"Son, I think those antics had little to do with Stanley and a great deal to do with one Ben Nash."

"Ociee, let's go see your room," said Mae.

She put her hands on my shoulders and ushered me into the hall. Seems my sister-in-law was changing the subject for Ben's benefit.

"Yours is the first on the right."

I pushed open the door. *Gasp*. "Flowers! Mae, there's flowers on my wall, like my room on Charlotte Street!"

It didn't concern me Aunt Mamie's 'Ociee room' flowers were blue, while my new Memphis room flowers were pink. I took pleasure in new ideas. What had my aunt taught me? I'd underlined it in my journal. *One's nest must undergo change from time to time for the sake of art.*

"I am delighted you like the wallpaper, little sister. In fact, these pretty pink roses are the reason your papa selected this house. He said, 'I want my daughter to imagine she's living in a garden.' He thought of the roses as a reminder of your mama."

I didn't know what pleased me the most, her mention of Mama, or Mae's calling me her 'little sister,' or my papa's picking the house just for me. I was happy, pure and simple.

Papa stuck his head in. "About as pretty as your room at Aunt Mamie's, isn't it?"

"Just as, Papa, IF not better."

"Uh oh, please don't be writing to Aunt Mamie hinting at such. Her feathers would ruffle. My sister takes pride in her decorative skills, being the expert seamstress she is."

"It'll be our secret, Papa."

I liked having a secret between Papa and me. Gracious sakes alive, if one more good thing happened, I'd swell up and bust.

*

"ANYBODY HOME?" The robust voice almost knocked me to the floor. Our brother's friend, a big man named Jim, stepped inside. Fred walked from the kitchen, extending his hand.

"Perfect timing, Jim. Mighty nice of you fellows to come tonight. Sorry it's late."

"It makes no nevermind to us, Fred. You know I'm close by on Linden. Figured your family could use extra help this evening, so I brought along my brother Charlie."

"How do."

"Thanks for coming."

"Glad to."

I peeked from behind my door, but leaned out too far and fell at their feet.

Ben raced in from his new room. "My room has three windows. I can see the moon through all of them!" Seeing two strangers, Ben asked, "Who are *you*?"

Fred responded, "Ben, these gentlemen, Mr. Jim and Mr. Charlie, are brothers. Mr. Jim, our neighbor and another Illinois Central man, and has already helped us get the house in order. Mr. Jim, Mr. Charlie, this would be my curious and not so subtle brother Ben. Crumpled on the floor is my sister Ociee."

I was embarrassed. I giggled, not saying a word.

Papa walked in. "Jim, Charlie, I'm George Nash."

"Pleasure, sir. Fred's always talking about his family," responded Jim. "Glad you made it to Memphis."

"Mr. Jim, Mr. Charlie, Fred got bit by a copperhead!"

"Enough for now, son." Papa frowned in a teasing manner. "I want to thank you. It's been a long three days for Fred, the children, and me. I sincerely appreciate your assistance."

Getting to my feet, I asked, "Papa, can I tell them about the Madstone?"

"I'm afraid your story will have to wait, Ociee."

I was only trying, as Aunt Mamie instructed me, to make interesting conversation for our first guests. Papa didn't care about manners, he wanted to unload our things and send Fred and Mae on their way.

"Ben," I whispered, "Let's help."

"All right."

He didn't mean to, but Ben tripped Mr. Charlie as the men were carrying in our dining room table.

Fred frowned and assisted Charlie to his feet.

"Sorry, Mr. Charlie."

"No harm done."

Ben was getting in their way, but not me. I kept using my best manners, carried smaller boxes inside, and made the men feel appreciated by chatting with them while we worked.

I followed Mr. Jim to the wagon.

"You're with Fred's railroad. Are you trying to become an engineer, too?"

"No, afraid not, little lady."

Mr. Jim, Mr. Charlie, Fred, and Papa had carried in the beds, three chests, and our trunks along with several boxes and the kitchen chairs. I assumed he needed a break.

"I'm sorry, Mr. Jim."

"About what, young lady?"

"Because you can't become an engineer."

Fred heard, put down a stack of quilts, and sighed.

"Ociee, Mr. Jim works with figures for the railroad. Like Papa, he's really good in arithmetic."

"I can work with figures," I said, excited we had something in common.

"Ociee, go to the kitchen, *now*!" Fred ordered. "I'd like for you to unpack the glasses, you remember, in the box marked 'Fragile,' and please bring us some water. Take Ben with you."

"Yes, sir!" I was pleased to have something important to do to, although I didn't like Ben helping me. I understood Fred was trying to get rid of him because he was in the way.

*

Papa insisted Fred and Mae leave a few minutes later, saying they'd already worked so late. Because they lived out close to the railroad, they had a fifteen-minute buggy ride ahead. I was afraid they'd be lonesome, but Fred said I shouldn't be concerned.

"Good night! If you miss us, come on back."

Fred didn't answer. I think he was kissing Mae. Ben agreed. He wrinkled up his nose and stuck out his tongue.

By the time Mr. Jim, Mr. Charlie, and Papa finished unloading, Papa's pocket watch read 10 o'clock. I'd been up late only once before, New Years Eve, December 31, 1899. I'd tried with all my might to stay up past midnight to greet the new century. I woke up the next morning.

"Get ready for bed, children. I'm going to check on Maud and Mule."

Ben went to his room. I went to mine. Because of the wallpaper, my room was already beautiful even without my things. As soon as I opened my traveling bag, I reached for Mama's picture.

"Here's my bedroom, Mama." Holding her picture, I turned slowly, showing her. "All that's missing is you. I hope you're content in Heaven tonight, but can a mama be happy without holding her children?"

I opened my journal. I had to write something on our first night. The only energy I had left was barely enough to make notes. I numbered every major event.

All of Abbeville turned out to say goodbye
Ben gave Tiger to Mrs. Adelaide, he was unselfish
Met Grannie Dot and Samuel Caldwell, and the Wrights
Miz Annie Kate Milam
Copperhead bit Fred
I saved Fred with Milam Madstone
Fred told me about Saint Agnes
Saw horseless carriage and MEMPHIS
Mae welcomed us home on East Pontotoc
Pink rose wallpaper
I love Mae almost as much as Papa, Fred, and Ben.

I stopped there, didn't want to think any longer or I'd wake up. Tomorrow would be another day full of things to get done. I didn't put on sheets. I crawled onto my bed and wrapped up in Mama's quilt. Papa walked in.

"Angels on your pillow, sweet girl," he said kissing my forehead.

"And on yours, Papa. I'm glad we're here."

"So am I, Ociee."

"Night, Ben!" I called.

No reply. I hoped he hadn't gone out through a window, but I was too sleepy to look in on him.

I closed my eyes and smelled lavender in the air. "Good night, Mama." I welcomed myself to Memphis.

Chapter 12

I slept sound as a stone. I'd only turned over once, snuggling comfortably in my own bed when the fear-filled smell of smoke alerted me. My eyes flared open.

"Where am I?"

"Asheville? The Murphy's home is on fire. NO, not again! I can't bear another dreadful loss!"

"Elizabeth, where are you?"

I was running, or trying to. Both my feet felt like tree stumps rooted deep in dirt. The Murphys! I couldn't let them down. They counted on me. I struggled to release my feet. I kicked off the quilt and sat up in my bed.

My bed?

"Where am I?" Home? Pretty pink roses surrounded me. The smell of smoke wafted through the air. Still dark, I slide out of bed and felt my way into the unfamiliar hallway.

"Drat!" I stumbled over an unpacked box.

"Ociee?"

"Papa!"

He lifted me to standing. "Are you all right?"

"Yes, sir, but I'm scared. Papa, I'm real scared."

Papa's arms encircled me. "I got you, sweet girl. You're safe with me."

I believed him, for then anyway.

Ben staggered from his room. I could hardly see the outline of his body as he rubbed his sleep drained eyes. "What's happening?"

"There's fire somewhere nearby, but not too close," assured Papa. "Stay put, children."

Ben and I did not obey. As our papa stepped out on the porch, we followed close at his heels. Other neighbors were running down our street. Someone pointed behind our house.

I turned around. In horror, I saw huge flames licking the blue-black sky.

"Papa, look there! We're not safe. Not safe at all! "

"Yes, you are. Trust me, Ociee. Now hold on to your papa and be your bravest."

Terrified, I clung to him. He gripped both Ben and me in his two strong arms.

I wasn't feeling brave, not one bit. I was feeling little, and very, very frightened. Most of my bravery had been used up. Then, as if someone suddenly lighted a gigantic oil lamp, the April dawn started to overcome the night. Red, orange, and pink slashes painted through the blackness. I squinted to determine if the crimson colors were blessed morning rays or more of the horrendous evil fire.

"Orleans!" shouted someone.

The fire wagon roared up the corner street. Bells clanging, its three horses galloped as other town folks followed along on foot carrying buckets of water and firefighting tools.

"It's turning onto Vance!"

Papa, Ben and I ran with the people. I held tightly to my papa's hand. My mind shot me like a cannon ball to Asheville and the horrible night the Murphy's home burned to the ground. As much as I trusted Aunt Mamie, I was more assured by Papa's grip.

"The school's on fire," shouted one of the men.

"St. Agnes is burning!"

The first time I ever laid eyes on St. Agnes Academy, it was going up in flames. Smoke filled the air. A loud army of people were shouting and heaving buckets of water on what appeared to be a huge and handsome building.

All I could see for certain was a foggy blur of windows and doors with bursts of fire belching forth. In my eyes, the school seemed like an enormous castle being consumed by a fierce fire-breathing dragon.

Ben, wild-eyed, watched in amazement. I clung to Papa.

*

By the time the sun was up in full, the flames had been defeated. I noticed 15 or more girls, some very small, while others looked even older than me. A few cried, while a couple of them looked on, dazed. I saw Elizabeth's face on every head.

The group huddled near some trees with holy sisters tending to them. The nuns made me think of swans as they moved slowly among the children. Quiet and calm, they were spirit-like in their long, white robes as they floated about, caring for the girls. I'd write about this one day. It wasn't my shyness holding me back from talking to the girls. Somehow I trusted those nuns were all they needed.

The fire continued to hiss and spit as men poured water and chopped at pockets of burning rubble with their picks and axes.

Papa spotted Mr. Jim and offered to help.

"Mighty kind of you, George, but we about got things under control."

"Anyone hurt?"

"Nope, thank the good Lord for the safety of the children and those nuns. Not one of us volunteers is badly injured either. There's a cut here and there, a few burns. The men are mighty tired; goes with the job."

"How's the damage look?"

"Don't know for sure. The convent took the worst of it, the chapel, and underneath in the dormitory."

"Sure I can't be useful?"

"No George, not today," said Mr. Jim. "Don't you worry though, I'll be calling on you to join up with us."

"I'd be honored, Jim."

When we overheard, Ben and I charged over.

My courage returned with gusto. "I'll join you, Mr. Jim.

I've had experience with fires. My friend Elizabeth's house caught fire, I helped!"

"But I'm older and stronger," said Ben as he pushed me aside.

Mr. Jim stood there. He wasn't accustomed to our enthusiasm.

"Let's allow Mr. Jim to get back to work," said Papa. He guided us out of the way.

"I think we should go home and fix breakfast. Mae left us with biscuits and jam."

Ben thought about his stomach and followed behind our papa. My concern held me there.

"Papa," I called to him, "you know full well, I can lend a hand."

"Come on, Ociee," he motioned for me. "I know you want to help, so do I. Mr. Jim said they didn't need us."

Reluctantly, I gave in.

*

It was April 11, 1900. In the days following the fire, the newspaper articles announced classes would go on as usual. Damage was contained in the chapel, in the convent, and in the dorms for boarding students.

Papa, Ben and I read every word we could get our hands on. One of the Sisters of St. Dominic, Sister Mary Rose, had been the first person to discover the fire. The brave nun alerted her superior, Sister Raphael, who quickly called to Sister Bernadette, who was in charge of the children.

"Papa, are you sure none of the sisters or girls were hurt?"

"Ociee, I think not, but be patient and let me read on." He studied the paper. "No, not one single person was injured. Says right here, because Sister Bernadette lined up the children and calmly told them they were going to the chapel, she got them outside without incident."

He continued, "So, you see, the children didn't know

there was a fire until they saw flames blazing from the roof."

"Thank glory." I let go my long-held breath.

"Trusting Sister Bernadette, none of the girls were frightened or confused. Some of the little ones were carried from their beds in blankets."

I remembered how cold Elizabeth was after the Murphy's fire, so I was relieved to learn they had warm blankets.

"Look here, Papa," I said. "This says there was another fire at my school. It was way back in 1878. It was a dreadful, terrible one like the Murphys'. The whole school burned up!"

The displaced nuns and the boarding students would be relocated to another house on St. Paul, not far away. I made a note of yet another saint in my journal. So far I had St. Dominic, St. Peter, St. Agnes, and St. Paul. I surely hoped some day, there'd be a St. Ociee noted in some other person's journal.

*

Papa and I worked hard getting our house in order. Easter was Sunday. We set our goal to be finished by then. We invited Mae and Fred over to celebrate and to thank them for everything.

Ben mostly got in the way, but he saw himself as being useful. I let him think so. I was proud of Ben for not breaking any more dishes. I had him haul empty boxes for Papa to burn later. We weren't in a hurry to start a fire. Our neighbors had had enough burning for a while.

Mae came by. Fred was on a railroad run, and she was happy to have something to do. We let her cook for us while we did the real work. Try as I did, I continued to forget to say her right name.

"Rebecca, whoops, I mean Mae."

"Ociee, I'll be your loving big sister were you to call me Rebecca, or Mae, or Talula Balula."

"Talula Balula!" I about fell on the floor laughing.

Finally settled in, Mae was the festive blue ribbon trimming the Nash family package.

"Goodbye, Talula Balula," I waved as she drove her buggy down East Pontotoc. "See you and Fred for Easter dinner."

My sister blew me a kiss.

Papa and Ben were sitting on the porch. "Believe this is the first time Ociee's let me rest since we arrived," chuckled Papa.

"Or me," grumbled Ben.

"Aren't you glad you worked hard and we're done?"

"I'm thankful you won't be ordering me around anymore, Ociee. You keep forgetting I am your *older* brother."

I rolled my eyes.

Papa squeezed my hand, "Thank you, sweet girl. Our house is perfect."

I rested well that night, never moving an inch.

*

"The new Nashes will be here any minute," said Papa.

Vegetables, beans and potatoes, bubbled on the stove. My blackberry pie cooled on the windowsill. Edges burned black, sunken in the middle, the pie was ugly as a squashed armadillo.

Setting the table with our good dishes, glasses, and Grandmother Nash's silver, I carefully placed Mama's blue vase filled with yellow daffodils in the center of her best white linen cloth.

"All done, Papa. You said 'new Nashes'? Are we the old Nashes? You know Fred is much older than Ben and me."

"New is for newly married."

"And, Papa, we're newly moved!"

*

"Delicious rolls, Ociee." praised Papa. "Your rather curious-looking pie doesn't taste half bad."

"It doesn't taste half good either."

"Ben Nash, it's better than any pie *you'll* bake."

"Ociee, everything was delicious, AND beautifully presented."

"Thank you, Mae. Papa helped. Truth is, he did a lot of the cooking."

"Mama's favorite tablecloth," said Fred as he raised his glass. "Here's to Susan Alberta Milam Nash."

"Yes, here's to Bertie. Your mama would love everything about this day. Happy *first* Easter to the newlyweds, and welcome to Memphis for the rest of us."

After we ate our armadillo pie, Fred asked if he might take Ben and me for a ride.

"Please, Papa, please may we go?"

"Perhaps. Mae, could I convince you to help me clean up?"

"Papa Nash, it would be my pleasure."

Ben and I raced one another to Fred's buggy. I sat contentedly between my brothers. A soft breeze sent us on our way. I was sorry for Papa and Mae, but this afternoon ride with just the three of us had a sweetness all its own.

"I've made some notes."

Ben groaned.

"You'll be pleased, Ben." I unfolded my list of places and held it for both of them to read: *Mississippi River*, *opera house, Cossitt Library, Cotton Exchange, Peabody Hotel, and SKYSCRAPER*. I wrote skyscraper in capital letters to make certain we got by there.

"Good for you, Ociee. We'll go every place we can as time permits. I don't want to leave Mae and Papa for long."

Fred's buggy headed west to Lauderdale Street, across Beale, and south on Madison Avenue. Our heads turned back, forth and every which away as Ben and I attempted to take in everything. Maud pranced as if she'd been a city horse for her whole life.

"Lucky for us, it's a Sunday, Easter Sunday, so downtown won't be overflowing with people. Look there, a trolley."

"Wow!"

"Let's count how many we see."

"Nah, too much else going on."

When we turned onto Second and pulled in front of the Cotton Exchange, Ben's head went back, back, and back.

"Can't make out the top. Bet we'd look like a toy buggy from way up there."

"If you think that's tall, just you wait."

We rode on.

When we stopped again, Fred pointed up. "The D. T. Porter building. Ociee, Ben, that's the world-famous skyscraper I told you about. What do you think?"

"Gracious goodness. It's so tall it DOES scrape the sky! You think poor little birds fly into it?"

Fred chuckled. "Ociee, only you would worry about the birds. Believe me, Memphis has birds a plenty, especially pigeons. I've yet to come across the dead body of one."

"Ociee, birds keep away from Madison Avenue, from all these big streets," said Ben with authority. "These buildings are way too high for the smart ones. They stay mostly in the country."

"Here comes another trolley."

When we passed the Peabody Hotel, I made Fred promise he'd take me inside another day. I pledged to spend a night or two, once I got grown. Later, I'd make a note to remind myself.

Fred slowed Maud as we approached the library on Front Street.

"My goodness, it's a palace!" I squealed. "Looks like the fairy castle in my storybook. Fred, you said I'd have to live inside there forever to read all their books. I wouldn't mind a bit."

I thought we'd seen it all but when we stopped in front of the opera house, I believed I had been dropped from the sky into London, England. Surely the royal family was about to step out onto the balcony.

"Look up toward the top," I said, pointing to the windows above the balcony. "Carved in the stone, 'Grand Opera House.' One day I'll come here."

I'd never seen as many beautiful churches, except in Asheville. There was a church for every faith I knew about. I was reminded of Asheville several times during our tour, but I hadn't wanted to hurt Ben's feelings by talking about my adventures in front of him. Ben was in high spirits.

We hitched Maud and strolled around Court Square with other folks in their Easter finery. Some rested on benches while others played with their families. In the center of the tree filled park was a massive, two-tiered fountain with a sculpture of a lady balanced atop. She watched over angels and children who were dancing in her water. It was a magical place.

"Please, Fred, will you take us to the Mississippi now? We've seen everything else on Ociee's list."

"Would you be willing to settle for a quick look? To truly enjoy the river takes a whole afternoon."

As hard as it was for me, I sided with Fred. "Ben, we can't leave out Mae and Papa, not on Easter."

"Well, all right."

Any disappointment Ben or I felt totally disappeared once Fred pulled onto Cobblestone Landing.

"It's an ocean!" Ben couldn't contain himself. He ran like a crazy person, stopping just short of plunging into the Mississippi River.

I wasn't any better. "I'm Christopher Columbus," I shouted. "I'm discovering America!"

Fred attempted to correct me, instructing us about Marquette and Joliet, and mentioning the 1660s. Ben and I were way too occupied counting riverboats and waving at people to pay him any mind. After a while, Fred said words we dreaded.

"Time to go."

We pretended not to hear.

"Ociee, Ben, we need to leave now." Trying not to lose his patience, Fred coaxed us with an ideal approach. "How about a trolley ride?"

"YES!"

A few minutes later, Fred secured Maud as Ben and I charged to the first trolley we spotted. With eyes round as dinner plates, we climbed on board. We rode two blocks and back. Ben and I were in paradise.

"Thank you, conductor man," said Ben. "This was the best ride of my whole entire life."

"You're welcome, young man."

"Happy Easter."

"Same to you, young lady."

Late Sunday night, I wrote about our adventure. Papa had to come in and put out the candle.

"You know the angels on my pillow, Papa? Some of them spend their days at Court Square playing in a beautiful fountain."

"I'm sure they're here ready to rest with you now, Ociee. Good night."

*

Bright and early Tuesday morning, Papa put on his suit. I wore the dress Aunt Mamie made me for Fred's wedding.

I could almost hear her voice. "Ociee, darling child, this is not a formal occasion. Pink satin is too fancy for the morning hour."

But Aunt Mamie wasn't there, and I wanted to wear my very best outfit for my first visit inside St. Agnes Academy.

"Ociee, please don't wear the hat," said Papa. "It's filthy with road dust."

"But this is my traveling hat. It gives me courage."

I looked in the mirror. Papa was right. My dress looked like it belonged to a princess, but with my hat on, I was a princess who was going catfishing.

I tossed my hat outside to sun and took Papa's hand. He and I walked toward Orleans Street. At Vance, we turned the corner.

I tried to conceal my bashfulness. Aunt Mamie taught me how to smile pleasantly and put on a confident face. She maintained, "Do as I say, dear, and no one will notice your timid nature."

Today I was brave for real, inside and out, no pretending necessary. It was either because I'd observed the sisters at the fire or that Papa was holding my hand. We climbed up the big staircase. He held open the heavy front door as I stepped inside.

It felt like one of the biggest steps of my life.

Chapter 13

"Welcome, Mr. Nash, Miss Nash. I'm Sister Bernadette."

"Sister Bernadette, I saw your name in the *Commercial Appeal*! You're a hero of the fire!"

The nun's long white robe, her 'habit,' stood out all the more against her bright red face. "It was the Lord who rescued the children, young lady. Not I."

"The LORD?"

Papa turned me around so I was looking directly into his eyes. He whispered, "Ociee, calm yourself. This is a quiet, humble nun. You must show respect and allow her to speak to you before you speak to her."

I could feel my face turning the same red as the nun's. I didn't know how I was supposed to act. As Papa suggested, I'd keep quiet.

Another holy lady came up. "Mr. Nash, Miss Nash, this is Sister Cecilia."

"How do you do," said Papa, being extra polite to show me how. Usually my papa is outgoing and shakes a person's hand. He must have been afraid to touch any part of the nun. Papa nodded at her. I thought he nodded for too long.

Sister Cecilia leaned down to me, tilted her head, and smiled. "You must be Ociee. Miss Small wrote us a glowing report about your aptitude."

"Yes, ma'am. I work real hard in school. My arithmetic and spelling are almost always perfect."

Sister Bernadette corrected me. "Say 'Yes, sister.'"

"Yes, sister. As I said, my spelling and arithmetic are pretty good."

I'd already messed up twice, and we'd only been in St.

Agnes a few minutes.

I'd do better. I about strangled on the words trying to work their way out of my mouth. I wanted to ask about the school, the other girls, and certainly about the terrible fire. Gracious goodness, I suddenly understood Ben and how difficult it was for him to stop talking.

"Your dress is lovely, Ociee."

"Thank you, ma'am, err, Sister Cecilia."

I wanted to tell about Aunt Mamie, her being a gifted seamstress, and about Fred and Mae's wedding. Papa told me to be respectful and quiet. I cupped my hand over my mouth.

"Ociee, are you ill?"

"No, I'm trying not to talk."

I discovered sisters could laugh. I believed persons as holy as these must walk around whispering and praying most of the time. I sure had much to learn about Dominicans.

Sister Bernadette instructed us to follow her. We entered a large room with a tall ceiling. It reminded me of Mr. Murphy's office with its fine furniture and heavy walnut bookcases. There were many unusual things hanging on the walls, including a crucifix behind the desk. Every time I looked at it, I felt awful sad.

I saw pictures of people from the olden days, mostly saints, I assumed, both men and ladies. I wondered if one might be St. Agnes.

A bell rang. Papa's head jerked.

"Fire!" I yelled.

"No, dear! Seat yourself," said Sister Bernadette. "I pressed this button to summon one of our students. She'll be here in a moment."

I noticed the two nuns were giggling. If I wasn't allowed to talk, I was pleased I could bring some merriment into the school. On second thought, I didn't want to behave like one of those dreadful troublemakers at my old school, who annoyed Miss Small.

There was a knock at the door.

"Come in, Agnes."

My mouth flew open. I whirled around in my chair, stood straight up, and exclaimed, "Are you Saint Agnes?"

Sister Bernadette all but collapsed. This time it was she who cupped her hand over her mouth.

Sister Cecilia clapped her hands together and raised her eyes toward Heaven. I assumed she was thanking the Lord for sending His saint to visit us.

The pretty young lady stared at me.

"Why no! I'm Agnes McCarney."

I thought Papa would pass out on the spot. "I'm sorry, Sister Bernadette, Sister Cecilia, Miss McCarney. I'm afraid this is our first experience with a Catholic school. There's much my daughter and I need to learn."

"I'm sorry, too. Reckon I was excited to meet a saint. My brother Fred has been telling me about St. Agnes, St. Dominic, St. Peter and . . . "

Before I completed my list, Sister Bernadette stopped me. "Dear girl, you certainly have an enthusiastic nature."

"Indeed," added Sister Cecilia. "We'll ask Agnes, she's the student, not the saint, to show you around our school. She's one of our finest senior students. Try to think of her as your guardian angel for a morning. Agnes will watch over you as would an angel, while we discuss your admission with Mr. Nash."

"Guardian angel?" I looked up at Agnes. "I know a Gypsy, but you're my first real angel." I recalled Papa's advice. "Never mind."

I didn't want this senior girl thinking I was stranger than she already did.

*

Agnes began by showing me two of the classrooms where I'd be. The girls were at recess. I wandered around the empty room, carefully touching a desktop and the back of one of the chairs.

"Our whole school in Abbeville would fit in this one room."

"Oh my word," exclaimed Agnes. She had never attended a country school. *Too bad for her*, I thought to myself.

I also told her about Asheville and Miss Small, so she would know I'd traveled. I was trying to impress her. Two girls my age came toward us.

Agnes asked them to stop and meet me.

"Ociee, this is Mabel Miller."

"Hello," I almost curtsied. Thankfully, I stopped my self.

"Very nice to meet you, Ociee."

Mabel said my name perfectly. Sometimes folks made fun of my name because Ociee is different; it's not like Mabel.

I got tired of explaining Ben couldn't say Josie when he was real young. Josie, short for Josephine, was another one of those pet names my family made up. Josie turned into Osie. Because Papa wanted me to be unique, he decided to spell my name the way we do now, O-C-I-E-E.

"And this is Betty Higgins."

"I really like your dress," she said.

I was proud as could be when Betty noticed. So had Sister Cecilia. Too fancy or not, I was glad I'd worn it.

"Thank you, Betty. I hope we'll become friends."

The way she smiled back at me, I thought we would. I thought about Elizabeth. She'd always remain my best friend. Actually, Betty could be short for Elizabeth. Maybe Agnes, my guardian angel, knew and made sure I got to meet a Betty. We saw several other older students in the hall. One person I met was Tillie Whitman. She had an unusually sweet look about her.

We toured the school, all three floors, and the beautiful grounds with many trees, oak, even apple, more than I could count. We sat for a few minutes on an iron bench and watched the sun dance in shadows on the soft green grass.

I felt comfortable asking Agnes questions. She told me she didn't really mind wearing the students' dark uniforms; said it was easier for her not to have to plan her wardrobe each night.

Agnes admitted she didn't mind being in a girls' school. When I questioned her, she replied, "Without young gentlemen around, I find it a more appropriate atmosphere for study."

I mentioned the mean boy who dipped my pigtails in the ink well. Agnes laughed, "You'll have no mischief here. The sisters are very stern about proper decorum and seriousness in the classroom."

I didn't quite understand what Agnes meant, but I knew full well my hair was safe.

As Papa and I walked home, we discussed our visit.

"Papa, my school has almost as many rooms as Abbeville has churches and stores. It's so big, I may get lost."

"You'll be watched over. While you were touring, I interviewed the sisters. I have it on their good word they've never misplaced a young lady."

"Papa, you're teasing."

"Maybe."

"I like really like St. Agnes and Agnes Agnes, too."

"Agnes Agnes!"

We laughed together.

"Good. Seems Fred knew what he was doing selecting this school for you."

As we strolled down Orleans Street, Papa started to whistle.

"Agnes spoke to me about what she called an 'important

principle' of our school. At first, I thought she was talking about Sister Bernadette."

"Isn't she?"

"No, Papa. Wait, you're teasing me again. I know it."

"You caught me."

"As I was saying, Agnes said every girl is trained to become a well mannered, educated young lady. Exactly what you and Aunt Mamie want for me."

"Absolutely, Ociee."

"I'm trying, Papa."

I know, sweet girl. Say, you don't have to become a well-mannered OR educated lady this morning. Come on, I'll race you home!"

There we were, Papa in his suit, me in my pink satin dress. We ran up East Pontotoc fast as we could go.

It was a perfect morning.

Chapter 14

Clear as day, there were *two* Ben Nashes climbing in our magnolia tree. One dressed in dungarees; the other wore brown pants.

The first Ben hit the ground in front of me.

The second Ben came so close I felt a rush of air as he landed.

"Look out, Ben, you about crashed into me. Can't you see I'm dressed up?"

"Why do you think I landed where I did?"

He was showing off for the other Ben, who was then standing shoulder to shoulder with my brother, glaring at me. On closer inspection, the real Ben didn't have near as many freckles and stood a tad taller.

Hands on my hips, I glared back.

Papa put out his hand. "Hello, young man, I'm Mr. Nash, and this is Ben's sister, Ociee. Who might you be?"

"Name's Billy Boy. Billy Boy Williams. I live three doors down."

"Nice to meet you, Billy Boy."

"I'm going inside. Don't want anything to happen to my dress," I said with an air of pride. "But I'm coming back."

"Don't hurry."

"Ben, watch yourself," said Papa.

I stomped up the steps.

Papa followed after me to work on his Draughons studies. I carefully hung my dress and put on clothes for play, dungarees like Ben.

"Going outside, Papa."

"You children be careful."

The door slammed behind me. "Sorry, Papa!"

*

"Ben? Billy Boy? Where did y'all go?"

I looked up in the magnolia, down toward Orleans, and around the back of our house. They were nowhere to be seen. I finally spotted them behind a house catty cornered across our street. They were running, laughing like the two goofy boys they were. I tore out after them.

"You're fast," panted Billy Boy. I had him by his shirttail.

"Fast for a girl," my brother teased.

"No, Ben, she's plain fast."

I let go Billy Boy's shirt and tried to keep from grinning.

"Want to go see what kind of trouble we can find?"

"Sure do!" Ben and I exclaimed in one voice.

It was a good thing Papa had his work to keep him occupied, or he'd have gotten worried. Ben, Billy Boy, and I were gone exploring until right before suppertime. Billy Boy showed us a curious old shed and houses where other children lived.

"There used to be two boys named Loftin and Emmett in the brown house," Billy Boy said, "but they moved to a great big house over on Monroe."

He told us there was a pond not far away and promised to take us fishing. Billy Boy showed us great hiding places, too, and a nice spot to play ball and hoops.

"And up thata way are some trenches. They're left from the War. Ma Gram explained about them when I showed her what I'd found."

"What did you find? A treasure? I found a treasure, too!" I announced proudly. Ben acted like he wasn't listening. "Mine was silver coins, over $100 worth. I even gave a portion to Mr. Jealous here." I hooked a thumb at Ben.

"Ociee, you got lucky," Ben huffed. "I'd have found those coins if I'd wanted."

Billy Boy shrugged. "All I got was a mess of rifle shells and uniform buttons. Ma Gram made me throw away things belonging to Yankees. I didn't exactly get rid of them like she told me. I buried them out back behind our washhouse. I'll show them to you if you want."

I hoped Billy Boy would become a great friend to both of us, just like Elizabeth; except he was a boy. I figured two boys and one girl was a better combination for us. One girl can be friends with two boys easier than one boy can be friends with two girls. Besides, I'd find plenty of girl friends at school.

Billy Boy made Memphis come alive for me. As much as I liked our house, my room, my school, and going to see the river, all those beautiful buildings, the library, the Peabody and Court Square, learning about Billy Boy's places was the kind of fun I prized.

Ben and I didn't have any idea where he was taking us as we wandered up and down, around and around the neighboring streets. I tried to remember: there was Walnut, Dunlap, so many names. Ben and I followed our new friend wherever he led. We started across Linden. I recognized that street. We'd driven in on Linden last week.

"Look out!" Billy Boy threw his arm across my chest.

A horseless carriage roared past.

"You got to watch 'em. They won't be looking out for you, too busy trying to control their motorcars!"

"I'll get me a ride some day," said Ben.

"Me, too."

"I already had one," said Billy Boy.

"You DID?"

"Yep."

"Tell!"

"Please, Billy Boy, we want to hear."

Billy Boy sat Ben and me down in front of what appeared to be an abandoned house. Grown up in tall weeds and massive vines, its thick-leaved trees and untrimmed bushes hid most of the two-story building. In what windows were visible, curtains were drawn. A chill ran straight through me. The dark, dreary house loomed behind us. It was a stranger's property in a town brimming with strangers.

"Ben?"

"Shhhh."

"All right."

Uneasy, I yearned to hear Billy Boy's account.

"Come on, Billy Boy," pleaded Ben. "You said you rode in the motorcar."

"Once Ma Gram rented a room to a lady, Miss Ruby, I think because she had real soulful brown eyes. Anyway, Miss Ruby had a gentleman friend, a fellow named Quincy, a tall skinny redheaded man. It's Mr. Quincy who gave me the ride. He allowed me to wear his own leather hat and some goggles so I wouldn't get dust in my eyes."

We were clinging to Billy Boy's every word.

"Mr. Quincy drove real fast. That's how come I warned y'all to watch out. I know how they drive, Mr. Quincy, anyhow."

"You gonna ride again?" I asked hoping we could go along.

"Nope. Miss Ruby up and married Mr. Quincy, maybe because he had a motorcar. I don't know. That's what Ma Gram said. Those two have been gone for a month or more."

"Dern it all," said Ben.

Ben had a way of saying exactly what I was thinking

"Ben, you're not supposed to say 'dern'."

"Yea, I know. It just shot out of me."

"I won't tell."

"Thanks."

I leaned back into the lower branches of a magnolia tree. Not only were we making ourselves at home on some stranger's property, but I also had no clue how we got there.

I attempted to soothe my uneasiness with an image of Elizabeth. How I missed her and the fun we always had. I wondered if her mother had given in yet and let her ride in Mr. Murphy's motorcar. Wished she and I were riding around this very moment; I'd know exactly where I was in Asheville. Didn't really matter though, Elizabeth, the motorcar, her parents, and Asheville were miles and miles away.

Ben was poking around the yard. It gave me freedom to talk to Billy Boy without my brother's infernal interrupting.

"Who's Ma Gram?"

"My Grannie."

"Why do you call her Ma Gram?"

"Because she's my Ma and my Grannie."

"How come?"

"My real Ma went missing."

"Is she dead?"

"Nope, just missing."

"Maybe she'll come back? Ours won't. Mama's dead."

Billy Boy had been half squatting, but he settled nearer to me and said, "I'm sorry for you, Ociee. Reckon your situation is worse than mine. My Ma might show up one of these days."

"I bet she would if she knew how nice you are."

The very second I said it; I turned six shades of red. Thankfully, Billy Boy paid no attention. I didn't want him to think of me as a girl.

"You're lucky you got your Papa. Ma Gram said I never had one of them."

"How come?"

"Don't really know, Ma Gram always stops herself from saying anything if anybody inquires about Buell something or other. It's like she needs to gripe, but instead she grabs her Bible and goes to praying."

The house's front door swung open. A hideously

wrinkled woman stomped onto the porch; a dark purple robe flowing behind her scattered leaves in its wake. The woman's wiry, gray-white hair was so long it touched her heavy black boot tops. She waved a long sword, "Get out of my yard THIS MINUTE!!!"

Ben was closest to her. "Run for it! She's a witch!"

"I'll witch YOU!"

We didn't stop running until we crossed Linden.

"Gotta stop," said Billy Boy leaning forward, his hands on his knees.

"Me, too," I said.

Ben stopped but not because he was out of energy. He rarely got tired. My brother wanted to stay close to us. He was so scared his light green eyes had disappeared into solid black pupils.

I was breathing too hard utter a word. My chest was heaving. The three of us stood in a circle looking one to another.

Exhausted, Billy Boy panted, "Let's, let's head on back. Ma Gram will have my hide."

"Who WAS that?" I asked. All I could think of was returning to our side of town, to Papa, near St. Agnes and those white-garbed sisters, who posed no threat. I hadn't been as frightened since Ben and I ran from the Gypsy.

"The witch woman scared me more than my Gypsy!"

"What's a Gypsy?"

"Billy Boy, Gypsies are scary people who roam around Mississippi in huge wooden wagons trying to capture children. They'll boil you in a big pot, if you aren't careful," answered Ben.

"For pity's sake, Ben. You know better!" I was over the moon furious. "Don't believe a word my brother says about Gypsies. He's jealous because a Gypsy man became my friend, not *his*. He was camped near our farm. Ben and I were spying on him when he noticed and came running after us."

I took a breath, "Papa said he had every right to chase us because we were bothering him. Anyway, I dropped this as we ran away. See." I showed him Mama's locket. "When the Gypsy returned it we became friends."

"Wow."

"Ociee talks about *her* Gypsy all the time. You'll get tired of hearing about him pretty quick."

Billy Boy paid no mind to Ben's warning. "Ociee, I never heard such a great story. Wish a Gypsy would come to Memphis."

"Could happen. My brother was wrong about the Mississippi part, too. Our papa said there are Gypsies all over the world. I'm sure most are every bit as nice as other people because Papa said so. He told Ben and me we can't be judging people in a bad way simply because they don't look like us."

"You can stop preaching any time now, Ociee," said Ben, his nose not two inches from mine.

"You're plain jealous, Ben Nash."

"Am not!"

"Are, too!"

"Y'all, quit!"

Stunned, we stared at Billy Boy in disbelief.

"Quit what?"

Billy Boy didn't have brothers and sisters, he'd told us while we were exploring. That was easy for me to believe when I saw how upset he got any time Ben and I started fussing.

"Y'all think that scary old witch woman might be like your Gypsy? Could she be nice?"

Together Ben and I shouted, "No!"

Chapter 15

We were a couple of streets over when we heard enormous clanging.

"Fire!" I was terrified.

"Fire!" Ben was thrilled.

"No fire, its Ma Gram's bell. It's how I know she wants me home. Billy Boy took off running like he was shot from Papa's pellet gun. Ben and I raced behind him.

We found Papa sitting on the front porch steps. "Where have you two been? You've been gone for hours!"

"Papa, we had fun exploring Memphis!"

"Billy Boy knows where everything fun is," added Ben. "He says we're just getting started."

We told Papa about what we saw and did. Almost. Without discussing it, neither Ben nor I mentioned the witch woman.

Billy Boy wasn't allowed to play with us again until the weekend. It suited me fine because I was starting to school in the morning.

Sister Cecilia welcomed me. "Ociee, I'm your teacher. Young ladies, this is Ociee Nash. She's from Mississippi AND North Carolina. You'll find your well-traveled classmate to be most interesting."

I looked at the nun wondering, for a second, who she was talking about. With sudden glee I said, "I AM very interesting!" Immediately I wished I could take back my words.

"As you can see, Ociee has a charming sense of humor." Sister Cecilia came to my rescue. Saying what I did would have forever marked me as stuck-up.

"I believe Agnes McCarney has already introduced you

to Betty and Mabel. Young ladies, please stand up. Ociee, take the seat between them."

We exchanged glances as the class began to murmur. Even though I'd gotten off on the wrong foot, I hoped they'd accept me. Being the new person in a school could go one way or the other, a lesson I learned in Asheville. Fortunately, Elizabeth had introduced me to her friends.

Thankfully, Betty did the same for me at St. Agnes. "Girls, eat lunch with Ociee and me. Mabel?"

"Yes, may I sit next to you, Ociee?"

"You may, Mabel." MAY, Mabel! I almost told Mabel about my new sister Mae, but decided against it. Instead I told everyone at our table about the Milam Madstone. Without doubt, I was viewed as *interesting*!

*

Sister permitted me to wear anything I wanted while waiting for my school uniform to arrive. At the start it was fun to stand out, but I would be relieved to match everyone else. I was also running out of clothes. My bridesmaid dress was way too showy for a regular St. Agnes student. I'd have to wear my calico every day.

Papa tried to help. He opened my trunk.

"Look here, Ociee."

He pulled out my silver velvet dress with green trim, the one Aunt Mamie made for our 'Turn of the Century' parade.

"I can't wear THAT, Papa! Any lady knows you cannot wear velvet after Easter."

"More wisdom from Aunt Mamie?"

"Leave the lady things to me, Papa, you've got your studies."

Folding my dress he said, "Want me to write 'Do not open until winter' on this?"

"No, thank you, I'll remember."

He closed my trunk.

"Papa, when I went to Asheville, I wanted to become a lady because you wanted me to, but now I want to become a lady for *me*."

*

I was a good match for St. Agnes, but Ben needed catch up work before he started to a Memphis school in September. While I was at school, Ben's tutor visited. It was a disaster.

"Ociee, that woman was ugly as a scrawny old turkey!"

"Ben, a teacher doesn't have to be pretty to be smart."

"Miss Brown was both. She's pretty and smart. Wish Miss Brown lived in Memphis."

"Me, too."

One day while we were at recess, Betty whispered, "Ociee, you fit in so well, it's as if you've been here all along."

"Must be the uniform." I looked down at the dark outfit. "I'm glad it finally came."

"No, Ociee, it's you. You're fun."

"And funny *looking*. That's what Ben says to me."

"I have a brother, he's eight. Boys can be awful, can't they?"

"Sometimes. Right now, I'm more concerned than irritated. It doesn't seem fair for me to be happy while Ben isn't, least not about his studies. He's trying to get used to a tutor."

"Your brother's not in real school?"

"Not until September."

Sister rang the bell. Betty and I lined up two by two to go inside. We usually picked one another as partners.

"Betty, do you think we'll ever get to wear white uniforms?"

"Why?"

"To match Sister Cecilia."

"Gracious no!" she replied. "Were we to match the nuns, we'd have to put on those awful long black veils."

"How awful!"

I'd miss feeling the wind in my hair.

*

"I knew that tutor woman was a mean one from the very minute Papa opened the front door."

"How, Ben?"

"Today she came in with a pile of books. They smelled bad, kind of like rotten grass, AND she carried a yardstick. The numbers were worn off midway down. I could tell she'd been hitting boys."

"I don't believe you."

"Ask Papa!"

I did. He sighed. "Ociee, the truth is the tutor didn't much appreciate Ben either."

*

Bright and early Saturday morning there came a loud knock at the door.

"What in the world? It's not yet 6 a.m.," said Papa. Ben and I had on our nightclothes and were just sitting down to breakfast.

Billy Boy burst through the front door, "It's Saturday! Get your clothes on. Time's a wasting, we gotta get going!"

"Want to join us?" asked Papa.

"No sir, Ma Gram already fed me and sent me on my way."

"I'm afraid you'll have to take a seat anyway, Billy Boy. My children must eat before they can play. They have to make their beds and do chores."

"I've done mine, Mr. Nash."

Papa indicated a chair. Billy Boy sat down. "Ociee and Ben tell me you live with your grandmother."

"Yes, sir. She says she's rough as a cob but loves me with all her heart."

Then, without being asked, Billy Boy repeated his story, the one he told us about his missing mama and his never-been papa.

"Reckon I'm blessed to have Ma Gram. She says so. She says we're blessed to have one another."

"Your Ma Gram sure has one loud bell," I said. "I about jumped out of my skin when she rang it the other day."

"That bell's left over from her teaching days. Ma Gram taught in a two-room schoolhouse back in East Tennessee before she moved to Memphis to raise me. Once she got here, she didn't much like my school and pulled me out. That's how come I'm learning better, according to her."

"I'll be," said Papa. He looked at Ben.

Ma Gram teaches me things I hadn't learned before, things about animals, trees and herbs, and birds. I know all about birds. In case you need to know anything, ask me."

He hardly took a breath.

"I still don't read well, not yet anyway. Ma Gram keeps trying to interest me in plays and poems, too. I AM good at figures. You know, arithmetic."

"I like arithmetic. Papa's good with numbers, too," I interrupted. "He's studying with Draughons. Right now he's working on bookkeeping."

"Maybe I'm not that good, Mr. Nash, but I will be. That's what Ma Gram promises."

"And I play a little music, too. When she came, Ma Gram brought along an upright piano. She hauled it all the way from Maryville, Tennessee!" he said, proud as could be. "To tell you the God's truth, Ma Gram and I go to battle every time she sets her mind on my practicing."

I was seeing another side of Billy Boy. Papa saw something else. He got up, excused himself and went to his room. Ben and I gobbled our breakfasts, all the time making our day's plans.

Papa came back with his fiddle. "Ociee talked me into bringing this with us. I thought I'd be playing it, but I've not found a minute."

"That's real nice, Mr. Nash. Could I show it to Ma Gram? She'd like to see it."

"Yes, Billy Boy. Maybe Ociee or Ben will go with you."

"We'll go!"

Billy Boy helped us with our chores. Papa poked his head in Ben's bedroom door, "Light is the task when many are the hands."

"May we leave, Papa? My chores are finished."

"Mine, too." It felt good to wear my dungarees after a week of stockings and dresses. I fluffed up my pillow and smoothed Mama's quilt.

"I'm going with you," announced Papa.

"You want to?"

Without a doubt, Papa's coming along would hold us back. Neither Ben nor I had mentioned the witch woman; we'd promised one another. That wasn't it. But what was he thinking?

"Why, Papa?"

He didn't answer.

Ben and I were puzzled as we set out down East Pontotoc.

*

"Ma Gram, I'm bringing company! It's the Nashes."

"Come on in," she hollered from the back. Our houses appeared to match, except their parlor was where my bedroom was.

As we walked inside, I smelled bread baking. I looked around. I'd never seen as many books! They were stacked and shelved and scattered about. An upright piano stood catty-cornered in the parlor. I could see through into the dining room where china dishes and silver pieces were displayed haphazardly atop a serving table and in a massive floor-to-ceiling walnut cabinet.

I was reminded of Aunt Mamie's. In truth, Ma Gram's home resembled Aunt Mamie's only had she NEVER tidied up.

"Sakes alive, our house is a mess," said Ma Gram as she wiped her hands on her apron. "But then, it always is. Please, make yourselves at home."

"Thank you," said Papa.

"Mr. Nash, so nice to meet you. And these are your remarkable children. I've been so anxious to get to know Ociee and Ben."

She took my brother's chin in her hands.

"Ben, you do look like my Billy Boy. He said your sister spotted the resemblance right away. Such a handsome young man are you!"

"Thank you, ma'am." Ben liked Ma Gram from that moment on.

"And this must be Ociee, what an appealing name. I've not heard it before. Is it from family?"

"Yes, ma'am, it's from *my* family. It's my name."

Papa corrected me. "Ociee, she means is yours a name that belonged to someone in our family."

"Oh."

"My daughter was christened Josephine, but we changed it a bit. Like her name, our Ociee is a first, she's unique."

I beamed.

"Let me get you folks something. Coffee? Juice for the children? Is anyone hungry?"

"No, but thank you kindly," said Papa.

"I feel a bit strange calling you Ma Gram," began Papa.

"I hardly answer to anything else, Mr. Nash."

"It's George."

"Then I must be called Ethelene. My name is Ethelene Williams. Billy is my grandson, but I'm more his mother due to unfortunate family circumstances."

"So we understand. He's an honest boy, very friendly, too."

"A tad too honest."

"Ethelene, that's another thing our children share in common. They all feel free to tell everything they know!"

"As my late mother would have said, 'and more besides.'"

"Sit down and have some coffee, George."

"I'm sorry, I really don't have time, Ethelene. I'm planning to work on the house today and I've paperwork to complete."

"Yes, I know about Draughons."

"Of course, you do!"

"Cream and sugar?"

"Ma Gram, we really need to get going," said Billy Boy.

"Only if that's acceptable with Mr. Nash."

"Of course. Have fun, you three. Be careful though."

"Off with you then! Be listening for my bell come lunchtime. You hear me?"

"Yes 'um!" Out we went. It was a glorious April morning, one alive with birds and the excitement of things ahead. There was a slight chill in the air as we hurried toward the witch woman's house.

Chapter 16

"Folks like the witch woman sleep all day. They get up late in the afternoon to creep around in the dark."

"It that right, Billy Boy? Ben, you must have waked her up last week. Reckon that's why she was so angry at us."

"Why's everything always my fault?"

"Now don't you two go to fighting. We have serious business here. I've been fearing the witch woman would figure out where I lived and come get me first, being that there's only one of me. Once she captured me and locked me in her house, she'd come after you two."

"I had a dreadful night dream about her," I told Billy Boy. "The witch woman was coming in through my front window. She tripped over my trunk and fell down. It made her so mad she started eating my foot."

Ben collapsed holding his stomach and laughing his fool head off. "You should have seen her, Billy Boy. My sister was hilarious. 'Heelllllp, she's got my foot! Help me! She's eating my big toe!'"

"Papa about broke his own toe getting to Ociee to save her."

"Ben Nash, you were scared a plenty, too, until you found out I was dreaming."

I was embarrassed he told Billy Boy about my nightmare. Worse still, Ben said, "Ociee, don't be a big chicken. Go on home if you're gonna act like a hare-brained girl."

"I am as fine as fine can be, Ben."

"I'm sort of scared myself," said Billy Boy.

"Well, I'm not," Ben insisted.

"Good, Ben. When we get there, you'll be the first to look inside."

My brother's bigheaded bragging stopped.

I wouldn't have let on for all the candy in Miss Ethel's candy store, but I was plenty afraid. The closer we got to the witch woman's house, the harder I breathed.

"There it is."

Gasp.

The house was bigger and darker and much creepier than the first time we saw it. Must have been because I'd seen the witch woman. How was it the sun was shinning, yet nighttime covered her trees and surrounded her house?

"Go on, Ben, peek inside," I said, half hoping he'd refuse.

"All right."

My heart hurt. Ben might get killed and it'd be my fault. Or at the very least, he'd be terrified out of his wits and become one of those folks whose hair turned white from fright.

Had somebody once scared the witch woman?

"Stop, Ben. I'm coming with you!"

"Shhhh," he whispered.

Billy Boy tripped over a tree root and fell flat, cutting his chin.

"Dag dog nabit!"

"Shhhhhhhh," said Ben even more emphatically.

I crept toward Billy Boy. "Your chin's bleeding. Does it hurt?"

"Nah, I get cut all the time." He pulled up his shirt collar and wiped off the blood.

We rejoined Ben.

"Let's spread out."

This was a true test of my courage. "I'm going this way." I walked off by myself. What I wished was for 'this way' to be straight back to my pink, rose-filled bedroom where night dreams would melt in a papa's arms. I crept slowly around the right side of witch woman's house.

Standing on my tiptoes, I carefully peeled down overgrown vines from her window. I pricked my finger on thick thorns and sucked out a fierce one stuck deep in my thumb. More determined than brave, I peeked inside. The window grime made it hard for me to see into the room. I used my handkerchief to wipe away the filth.

A sudden shudder chilled me bone deep.

There was almost no furniture except for a large dark red chair with curved legs and clawed feet. A dollhouse sat in the room's center. An empty cradle was shoved up against a fireplace piled deep with ashes. On a marble-top table next to the chair were a candle, a book, and a music box.

Were children locked inside? Hers? Would the witch woman kidnap one of us, Ben, Billy Boy or me?

My intense curiosity fighting my fear, I was drawn to a second window. Up on my toes, using a clean section of my handkerchief, I cleared another spot. An upright piano, similar to Ma Gram's, stood by a bolted door, almost if it prevented the wall from collapsing.

I could hear Ben's loud whisper behind the house. I moved toward the sound.

"Ben?"

A hand grabbed me. A tall form blocked the sun as long, yellowed fingernails dug into my shoulder. Consumed with fright, I slowly turned my head. The witch woman's silver hair gleamed in patchy light.

"I told you children to get away from here!"

I prayed the witch woman was just another awful nightmare. She was NOT. She was as real as her fingernails clutching me. Next I prayed to be back in Mississippi, in Asheville; to be anywhere but where I was!

"Papa!" I kicked the witch woman with all my might, but my foot got tangled in her smelly purple robe. Her wiry hair fell forward, brushing my face.

"Mama!"

"I ain't yo' mama," she growled, "My girl is dead and buried."

"Ociee!" Ben and Billy Boy raced from the back of the witch woman's house.

"Help!"

"We're coming!"

"Let go of my sister," Ben yelled, "you witch woman you!"

I broke free of her claw-like grip, and the three of us ran for our very lives.

"I ain't no witch!" She bellowed as we rounded the corner. "I'm an old woman who deserves her peace. Get out of here! AND don't come back!"

We ran three blocks without stopping. Exhausted, Billy Boy collapsed by a hitching post. Ben dropped down next to him, but I was still in a frenzy. I couldn't quit moving.

"I thought you were a goner, Ociee."

"So did I," said Billy Boy.

Pacing in circles around the boys, I said, "I feel sorry for her.

"WHAT! You feel sorry for the witch woman?"

"Yes."

"She about killed you!"

"No, she didn't, Ben. She about scared me to death, but she didn't try to kill me. Before you and Billy Boy came around the corner, she told me her girl died."

"Her girl died?" echoed Billy Boy.

"Yes, must be whose dollhouse and cradle I saw in the front room. They belonged to her dead child."

"What cradle? A dollhouse? Ociee, are you dreaming again?"

"No, Ben, when yawl went behind the house, I peeked in the window and saw a big red chair and the little girl's things."

"All we found was empty rooms," lamented Ben.

"Don't you see? She's NOT a witch at all. She's a sad old lady who wants us to leave her be."

"What about the sword? I didn't see her sword this time."

"Don't you understand? She recognized us. She didn't mean us any harm, or she'd have carried the sword."

"Ociee's right," said Billy Boy. "Some times folks don't like other folks. Ma Gram says that."

"Papa, too. He surely would want us to behave better than we have. He's gonna be madder than a wet hen once he finds out what we've gotten into!"

Ben, Billy Boy, and I explored around for another hour or two. He showed us his old school and another deserted house.

"Let's not go there yet," he joked.

"Why not?" Ben asked, heading that way.

"BEN!" we both yelled.

"I was just joking."

"Sure you were."

Ma Gram's bell rang. This time the sound was welcomed.

We walked inside with Billy Boy.

"You two want to stay for lunch?"

"Sure do," replied Ben.

"I thank you very much," I said, "but there's something I must do."

"I'm walking my sister to the door."

I couldn't believe Ben said that. I looked at him like he had three noses.

"Walk my sister to the door, my foot."

"I had to make sure you weren't blabbing to Papa about the witch woman."

"Ben, we will tell Papa. WE must. But I'm not telling him about the woman right now. Hear me, Ben, she's not a *witch woman*, she's a WOMAN."

"Yeah, if you say so." Ben's voice wasn't the least bit sincere.

"Stop it, Ben. Now have a nice lunch, and by all means, be polite. Don't talk with your mouth full, and remember to say your thanks to Billy Boy's grandmother."

"Yes, Aunt Mamie."

"For pity's sake, Ben!"

"Thank you, *Aunt Mamie*."

*

"I'm back, Papa. Ben is eating with Billy Boy."

"Yes, I know. I thought you'd stay for lunch, too?"

"No, Papa, I'm getting cleaned up. I've going for a walk."

Papa must have been concentrating on his studies. It wasn't like him to not question me. I was relieved. Ben was right about me blabbing to our papa. It was difficult for me to not tell him what happened. I washed my hands and face, applied salve to my thorn wound, and put on my calico dress. Again! I walked down the street to my school, where I found the gardener working in a flowerbed.

"Excuse me, mister. Where is St. Paul Street? Also, could you please tell me what I must do to speak with Sister Cecilia?"

"Well, little girl, you'll keep going on Orleans for a good long block, then you'll see a home, a good size home. Last week, I placed the sign. It reads "Convent of the Sisters of St. Dominic." The sisters are inside, but I wouldn't bother them. Can't this wait until Monday? By the way, you are a St. Agnes girl, aren't you?"

I thought a minute, then grinned. I already felt as if I belonged here. Indeed.

"Yes, mister, sure as sunshine I am."

Chapter 17

What seemed like a good idea at the time caused me to question myself when I spotted the sign: Convent of the Sisters of St. Dominic.

However, I was already there, so I reached for the bell. A lady answered.

"Excuse me, are you a nun?"

"No, I am not. What do you want here?"

I started to run away. Then I heard the sweet sounds of children singing. "Who do I hear?"

"Boarding students. Are you looking for one of our young ladies?"

"No, I'm looking for an older young lady, my teacher, Sister Cecilia. May I see her, please?"

"I'm afraid not, the sisters are in prayer."

"It's ever so important."

"So is their prayer."

"Reckon it is."

As I turned to walk down the steps, I spun back around. "Those boarding girls sure do sing pretty."

"Ociee Nash, what are you doing here?"

"Sister Cecilia!"

I ran up to her. "I have to speak with you, Sister. I know it's not allowed, you're praying and all, but something terrible has happened. I know I should tell my papa, but the only thing I could think about when the witch woman said what she did was getting to you!"

"Calm yourself, Ociee. Did you say 'witch woman'?"

"Yes, Sister Cecilia, except she's not really a witch. Ben, Billy Boy, and I thought she was because of her long silver hair and smelly purple robe. In truth, she's a dreadfully miserable person who's lost her little girl. I thought if I found her a new child, she might feel better. My brother Fred said St. Peter's Orphanage takes in children without families."

"Slow down, dear child. Please come inside."

"You'll let me?"

"Yes, Ociee, would you like a cup of tea?"

To my surprise, the inside of the convent looked like the inside of real people's houses. There was furniture, rugs, and shelves with vases and books galore. Even though books filled the rooms like Ma Gram's, the convent was as orderly as Aunt Mamie's.

As in Sister Bernadette's office, holy persons' images looked back at me. Another sorrowful crucifix reminded me I was grieving again. This time I mourned for the cheerless woman who missed her girl.

The sisters' cook was shocked to see me.

"It's quite all right, Carrie. Ociee is my student. She's come by for a short visit. We'll have some tea, please."

Thank glory Aunt Mamie taught me proper manners for a tea party. Otherwise, I'd have been lost when Carrie set the tea service in front of us.

"Would you like for me to pour, Sister?"

"How lovely, but no, I'll prepare your tea. Sugar? Cream? Lemon?"

While we sipped tea, I told her the entire story. I even mentioned Mama and how the Gypsy returned my locket. "See, isn't it pretty?"

"Indeed, it is. I noticed your lovely piece the first day you came to St. Agnes."

"You did?" Her praise pleased me beyond measure.

"Yes, Ociee, I can well understand your gratitude.Sister Cecilia, like my Gypsy, the scary lady could be good inside. That's the reason I need an orphan. I simply have to do something for her."

"My dear," Sister sipped her tea. "My heart goes out to

this poor soul."

I could tell the sister's concern was genuine by the tears welling up in her eyes.

"Fred told me the Dominicans have cared for folks in Memphis for years and years. He said the sisters nursed the War's wounded and those folks sick with yellow fever."

"Ociee, there's a very long history of suffering in this town and, yes dear, my order has been of service. Thankfully, the War finally ended and yellow fever has never returned. Praise be to the Lord."

I bowed my head "Amen. Is that the right answer?"

"Ociee, every child's prayer is the *right answer*."

As we talked, Sister Cecilia finally convinced me giving an orphan to the woman would not be the best thing for either of them.

"As I think about it, Ociee, I wonder if this woman lost her family either in the War or, perhaps, to yellow fever? I think it's possible."

"It's too tragic!"

"Ociee, you lost your dear mother to the measles epidemic. It's obvious the painful hurt remains deep in your soul. Perhaps your own loss could be one reason for your sensitivity toward this woman. You see her as a kindred spirit."

"Kindred spirit." Her words embraced me. "That's why I feel sorry for her?"

"Could be. Your tender heart explains your concern."

I appreciated Sister for saying my heart was tender.

"However, you are a young girl with much to learn. You must not act too hastily. The best thing you can do is pray for this woman. Hopefully, you'll be guided through prayer, to an appropriate way to console her. I shall remember you both in my own prayers."

"You *shall*?"

"Yes, I promise. Now, I'm sorry to say, you must go."

"Thank you, Sister Cecilia. Thank you for helping me. Thank you for the tea."

"You're welcome, Ociee."

As I hopped on one foot down the convent steps I prayed out loud. "God, while you are busy blessing, bless Sister Cecilia, too."

*

After dinner on Saturday night, Papa presented Ben with some news. "Son, I've found a solution for your schooling."

"Can't we wait until the fall?"

"No, Ben, WE can not wait until the fall. Ociee is in school, and I'll soon have a job. I'm not about to leave you here alone to get into devilment! We no longer live in Abbeville, where every one watches everyone else's children."

"Ociee! You told him, didn't you?"

"Told me what?"

"I did NOT!"

Papa scowled at us. "What's happened NOW?"

"Nothing, Papa. I promise. Nobody's hurt, and neither of us is in trouble."

Admittedly, I'd left out one thing. The witch woman. The boys and I had made her real mad and for a second time. Papa needed to know.

"Please, Papa, let's talk about Ben."

"You're trying to whitewash something. I know it as well as I know my name is George Nash."

But he let the subject drop for the meantime, and I sighed with relief. The April night was slightly chilly, so we stayed inside making use of our parlor for the first time. We sat at Papa's feet. I was on the footstool, while Ben sat cross-legged on the rug. Mama's portrait, the formal one not showing her smile, watched over us from above Papa's desk.

"It's safe to say St. Agnes is the perfect choice for you, Ociee. However, Ben, I'm afraid Fred didn't do as well with his choice for you. Don't go into another hissy fit about the shortcomings of your tutor. She's a dreadful woman. "

"Papa, you yourself call her a 'dreadful woman'! You must agree with me," cheered Ben.

"Reckon I do."

"I told you so!"

Nothing satisfied Ben more than being right.

"That said, I've found you the best teacher in town. You start Monday."

Ben moaned.

"Her name is Mrs. Williams, but she may allow you to call her 'Ma Gram.'"

"Ma Gram? Billy Boy's grandmother is going to teach me? Will he be there?"

"She teaches him, so I imagine you'll be working together; IF both of you can behave. We're fortunate she is qualified to do this, son. Ma Gram has years and years of experience. I expect you to be very respectful just as you were with Miss Brown."

"Yah whooo!"

I grinned at him. "I'm glad about Ma Gram, Ben."

I truly was. I knew two things for certain. First, Ben hadn't liked school until he met Miss Brown. Secondly, Ma Gram was a loving person who was smart and interesting and most of all, patient. From what Billy Boy said about her, she was the perfect choice for my brother.

"So, this morning, while you were out doing the Lord only knows what, I had a nice conversation with Ethelene Williams. She is pleased to take you on."

"Eth-E-leeeeen, no wonder she goes by Ma Gram!"

"Benjamin Nash, you will begin by NOT making fun of her name."

My brother realized he had crossed a line. He looked at

Papa and said, "Yes, sir. I'm making you a promise this very minute. I'll work as hard for Mrs. Williams as I did for Miss Brown."

Papa added, "I'm counting on you. Miss Brown sent all your reports to the tutor. I had the poor woman leave everything with me when she made her, hmmm, her abrupt exit."

"*Poor* woman, Papa, I thought you said she was dreadful?" I wanted to make everybody laugh again.

Papa didn't think it was funny the second time. Even so, Ben and I pinched at one another. Papa frowned.

"Next topic. What's making you two so antsy?"

I didn't want to erase Papa's satisfaction with Ben, so I decided to take the blame.

"Papa, I'll tell you the ending first."

He stretched out his long legs and folded his arms across his chest. I reminded him of my coming home to change into a dress.

"I should have known something was wrong right then," he said.

"Well, I'm glad you didn't stop me, because I had a grand visit with Sister Cecilia."

"With your teacher?"

"Yes, sir. She couldn't have been kinder. Even though she couldn't give the witch woman a new child, she offered to pray for her."

"What ARE you talking about? Who IS this witch woman?"

"I'm gonna start calling her 'the fever lady.' After Sister told me about the yellow fever and how it likely took her family, I can't call her a witch anymore!"

I tried to stop Ben, but my bullheaded brother jumped to his feet.

"The witch woman grabbed Ociee, Papa! Billy Boy and I had to rescue her. If we hadn't been there to save her, there's no telling if she'd be alive right now."

"Ociee, is this true?"

"It's true, and it's not true. She did creep up behind me. I was scared to pieces. First I hollered, 'Papa!' then I hollered, 'Mama!' That's how come I heard about her dead girl. We ran away as fast as we could. It's awfully sad, Papa."

He sighed.

"You know the rest. Well almost. Today was our second time to go over there. Last week was the first time she scared us off."

"Papa buried his head in his hands. "I should have suspected something when you had your nightmare."

"I dreamed she was eating my foot."

Ben chuckled. Not me, I never wanted to keep anything from our papa. I wished I'd talked to him from the start.

"I'm sorry, Papa."

"Me, too," said Ben, his own guilt surfacing.

"Ben, you stayed at Billy Boy's for lunch."

"Yes, sir."

"Ociee?"

I hung my head. "I went to visit Sister Cecilia."

"And asked the nun to give the crazy 'fever lady' an orphan from St. Peter's," said Papa, shaking his head.

"I did."

Our papa had been shaking his head so much in the last few weeks, I worried his brains might come loose and he'd not be smart enough to pass his business school tests. I wasn't concerned that fever lady would come and get me, but Ben wasn't convinced.

That night he came in my room after he thought Papa was asleep.

"You thinking about the witch woman?"

"She's the *fever lady*, Ben. I know she seems frightening, but in truth, she's sorrowful. Fever lady doesn't have people to care about her like us. I wish we could do something to brighten her life. Sister says to pray for her."

"I'm going to bed, Ociee. I'll pray for her, for her not to come get YOU!" My brother grabbed me and tickled me. We tumbled onto the floor. THUD.

Papa hit the floor running. "What's wrong in here?"

"Nothing, Papa, Ociee's just praying."

Our papa said not one word. He turned on his heels and went back to bed.

"Angels on your pillow, Papa."

"Ociee, I need a house full of angels to watch over you children."

Ben called, "I'm gonna do better, Papa."

"I'm sure you're trying, son. I'm sure you're trying."

A few minutes later, after Ben left, Papa came back in and sat on the side of my bed.

"Ociee, it gladdens me to know you care about others. Even so, I agree with Sister Cecilia. Lift the woman in prayer, but let that be enough. Do you understand?"

"I understand, Papa."

I crossed my fingers in case my prayers lead me to something more.

"Good night, Ociee."

"Good night, Papa."

"Good night, Ben."

"Can't hear you, Papa," Ben called from his room. "I'm sound asleep because I'm already improving."

Chapter 18

I couldn't get the fever lady out of my mind for trying. Sunday afternoon, we went down to Ma Gram's house to see if Billy Boy could play.

"Mrs. Williams," Ben asked, "can I still be friends with Billy Boy tomorrow when you become my teacher?"

"Weren't you friends with your school mates in Abbeville?"

"Yes 'um."

"Well then, there you are. Also, Ben, I will remain 'Ma Gram'. You're making things far too complicated than need be."

I looked up at her solemnly. "He promised Papa he was gonna reeeallllly behave."

"And you will, Ben, I'm sure of it," she said. "Would you children like some fresh-baked cookies?"

"Yes, please!"

"May I have two extra for a friend?"

"You surely may, Ociee, take four. There's a gracious plenty. Here's a piece of brown paper to keep them fresh."

Billy Boy picked up Papa's fiddle.

"Please don't break it!" I said, not meaning to sound so anxious. After all, it wasn't as if he was messing with the fiddle.

Ma Gram must have been concerned, however, because she watched Billy Boy like a hawk. "Ociee, would you like to learn to play? I'd be happy to teach you."

"Yes, ma'am. How grand. Papa will be thrilled."

"Shall we surprise him?"

"Think it's a good idea?"

"In my opinion, Ociee, surprises are almost always good ideas."

"Whew, what a relief," said Ben. "I was afraid *I'd* have to learn to play it. A boy's got more to do than sit around fiddling!"

Billy Boy agreed.

"Ociee, when do you want to begin?"

"Can we wait until summer? I'm busy with school."

"Perfect." She shook my hand. "We have a commitment."

"I'll *commit* to practice."

"I'll hold you to it."

*

As delighted as I was, I had one thing on my mind. I went home and asked Papa to let me take Maud for a ride.

"Only if you stay within a few blocks of home."

"I will. There's a park on the other side of Union. May I ride there?"

"Yes, but be back in an hour."

"I promise."

I put the cookies in Maud's saddlebag. At the end of our street, I turned right onto Orleans, took another right onto Linden, and left onto Dunlap.

The carefully crafted note in my pocket read: My brother, our friend, and I have been dreadful pests this week. I am writing to say I am sorry. If they knew I was doing this, they would say the same. I hope these cookies will bring you joy. O.N.

I wrote 'dreadful' because it relaxed me. Chuckling about Ben's tutor, I was less nervous while writing. I signed only *O.N.*, my initials, in case Ben was right about fever lady. If she was out to get me I didn't want her to know my name.

Without making a sound, I tiptoed up her walkway and placed the cookies outside the front door. The memory of those long, yellow fingernails shot through my body like bullets. I wondered if her nails had turned their grim color because of the fever. I raced off the property fast as a scalded cat. Riding home, I began to feel guilty. Though Papa had praised me for caring about fever lady, he had ordered me to leave her alone.

"Ociee!" Papa was standing on the porch waving some papers.

I panicked. Had he figured out where I'd gone? My heart racing, crushing guilt strangled me.

I slid down from the saddle and tied Maud to the hitching post.

Papa rushed toward me.

"I'm sorry, Papa, but I had to . . . "

"Here's the news of the century, Ociee girl!"

"Papa?"

"Mamie's gotten married!"

"Mamie who?"

"Your AUNT Mamie! She finally said 'yes' to George Lynch." He waved a letter in my face. "Here, Ociee, read it for yourself."

I *think* my papa lead me onto the porch. I was so dazed, for all I knew I floated up there on the afternoon's air. I sat on the porch swing, the message gripped in my quivering hands.

"Mamie's letter was actually delivered last week, but accidentally to Ma Gram instead of to us," he explained. "It took several days for her to come across it, because she only opens her own mail on Sunday afternoons."

I examined the envelope. The return address read:

Mrs. George Lynch
66 Charlotte Street
Asheville, North Carolina

Papa continued, "Embarrassed by the delay, Ethelene brought it to me right away. I heard her knocking with such fervor, I thought something had happened to Ben. She assured me the boys were being good as gold."

I was barely listening. My mind flitted around, thinking of all the times Mr. Lynch and I pleaded with my aunt to marry him. Because it was I who pushed them together in the first place, I'd figured the cause was lost when I left. Aunt Mamie's appreciating what a fine husband Mr. Lynch would make had seemed all the more impossible after I moved to Memphis. I couldn't imagine how Mr. Lynch finally won Aunt Mamie's heart without my help.

"What did you say, Papa?"

"I said Ethelene delivered the letter while you gone. She apologized over and over for the mix-up, insisting all the while she was going to get better organized."

I held up the letter from Aunt Mamie and read:

> *My dears, Ociee, George and Ben, Fred and Mae,*
>
> *I penned first your name, precious girl, for it was you who so adamantly encouraged my courtship with George Lynch.*
>
> *Do you remember, dearest, my mentioning a* <u>*surprise*</u> *when I wrote prior to your journey to Memphis? This is the news, my dears Ociee, brother George, Mae, Fred and Ben. We have another George in our family; ours now includes George Lynch.*
>
> *I understand this may come as a shock to everyone. Most certainly it has set tongues wagging in Asheville, given my advanced years. Only you, Ociee, and perhaps your father, will relish the delight in our union. I well remember the two*

Georges and how much they took pleasure in the company of one another during your father's visit here.

Alas our Ben has not met my charming husband. This letter is intended as a remedy. I have often yearned to better know Ben and Fred and to meet the lovely Rebecca. One correction must be made. I anxiously look forward to meeting one Mae Nash.

You must be trying to adjust to my words, but at your earliest convenience, George and I would like to travel to Memphis and spend some time with the Nash family.

Before I close, I must make one thing clear to all concerned. Even though George Lynch is now the proud owner of one of those loud and frightening motorcars, we will arrive by railroad for our own comfort and for safety's sake.

With my love to the family,
Mamie Lynch

I kicked out my feet out moving faster the porch swing "Papa, isn't this the most exciting news!"

"Sure took *me* by surprise. I always believed Mamie's plan was to remain an independent woman."

"She's independent, Papa, except Mr. Lynch has become part of her plan."

"Right you are, darling daughter. How right you are."

I thumbed back through the letter.

"Surely wish we'd been at the wedding, specially you and me, Papa. Why do you suppose we weren't invited? I could have worn my bridesmaid dress from Mae and Fred's wedding."

"I'm certain your aunt had no gathering whatsoever. She would consider doing so as improper."

"Improper?"

"Ociee, my sister is not a *young* lady."

"Well, she's NOT a man!"

"Ociee, that's not what I mean. Sorry to say, but Mamie Nash, my dear sister, is no spring chicken."

"All right then, Aunt Mamie isn't a man or a chicken, but that doesn't explain why she didn't want to celebrate."

"Ociee, please, write to your aunt and pose the question for yourself. I've got to get my studying done. By the way, I forgot to mention it, but I'll be starting my new post in less than a week."

"Post? Are you gonna work for the post office like Mr. Hightower?"

"No, Ociee! *Post* is another word for 'position.' I'll be working nearby at a mercantile store similar to Fitch's. I'm hoping to take you and Ben to meet the other workers once I'm situated. I'll become the main bookkeeper when I finish Draughons."

I hugged his neck. I'm proud of you, Papa."

"Thank you. Now write Mamie or I'll never hear the end of it. Get stationery from my desk."

"Yours, Papa?"

"Might as well. You'll need something nice because you are writing to a bride. My sister Mamie, a bride, who'd have thought it?"

My papa was right, he wouldn't hear the end of it until I got my thoughts straight. Not going to their wedding hurt my feelings, pure and simple. Aunt Mamie and Mr. Lynch would never have gotten together without my urging. I wrote a practice letter on scrap paper before I penned it onto Papa's nice stationery. I spent an hour, but every word I wrote came out sounding like I was unhappy about them getting married.

Congratulations, why didn't you invite us?

I'm happy for you, wish we could have come.

You finally said yes to Mr. Lynch. Why was I not there?

Happy marriage, Aunt Mamie and Mr. Lynch. My pink dress would have been the perfect thing for your wedding.

Piles of scrap paper blanketing my floor, I made one final attempt.

Dear Aunt Mamie,

We got your letter with the wonderful news about your marriage and your visit to Memphis. In the beginning, I was sad because we were not there. Papa said you were too old to invite people. I am planning a family dinner to celebrate your wedding. Next time Mae comes to see us, I will ask for her help. Mae is a good cook. Please write saying what you want to eat. I remember Mr. Lynch loves food.

We are happy here. At first, I was disappointed because I was not going to see you and everyone else in Asheville, Elizabeth, mostly. Please visit her before you come to Memphis. I want to know everything.

Papa is almost a bookkeeper. Ben has a nice teacher who lives on our street. I love my new school, St. Agnes Academy. It sounds real fancy because it is. Even so, the girls and the nuns are not snooty like

you and I always thought the Vanderbilts
in Asheville must be.
Please come quick as you can.
With love to Mamie and Mr. Lynch,
Your Ociee

I mailed my letter the next morning.

As for the guilt I'd felt about taking the cookies to fever lady?

Papa admitted he 'forgot to mention' his new job to me. So I did the same thing. I 'forgot to mention' taking the note and cookies to fever lady.

Chapter 19

Sister Cecilia glided by my desk, passing out our compositions from the previous week.

Even peeking as much as I could, I couldn't see any feet under her long white robe. She moved softly and quietly like a butterfly. What signaled Sister's presence were the endless black beads cascading from her waist. It was strange to me. Mama, Aunt Mamie, all the ladies I knew wore beads around their necks or wrists. I yearned to ask about Sister Cecilia's beads and why the tragic cross hung at the end, but I'd have to wait. Were I to speak to her, I'd surely confess to taking cookies to fever lady's house.

"Very nice work, Ociee."

"Thank you, Sister Cecilia."

I was thrilled to receive an "A" for my very first grade. I couldn't wait to show Papa. He was already home when I arrived. So was Ben. I waved my "A" in the air as I rushed inside.

"Good for you," said Papa. "You're off to a fine start."

"Ma Gram doesn't give grades. SHE gives hugs," said Ben.

"How encouraging, Ben." I meant it.

I had turned over a new leaf, in large part because of Billy Boy. When he noticed our bickering, I noticed it, too. Being more patient with Ben was a tough task for me because he could be very *irksome*. Sister had assigned us a new list of words to practice. "Irksome" was on her list. Ben Nash was a perfect example. I about chewed a hole in my tongue to keep from calling him "Benjamin Irksome Nash."

"I don't understand why Aunt Mamie refuses to come

in Mr. Lynch's motorcar," complained Ben.

"In the first place, Ben, we live far away," explained Papa. "Beside, driving a motorcar is a most dangerous undertaking."

I sat quietly practicing *serenity*, another word from Sister's list. I wanted Mr. Lynch to drive his motorcar to Memphis as much as Ben did.

"Mamie and George would be extremely uncomfortable bouncing around on those terrible dirt roads. I cannot imagine how hazardous the mountain trails might be," he continued. "Even horse drawn buggies turn over in the rough terrain. Try to imagine what might happen to people going fast."

"Sounds exciting!" said Ben.

Visions of Aunt Mamie and Mr. Lynch in an upturned motorcar popped my serenity like a soap bubble.

"More importantly, should their motorcar break down along the way, there would be no help for them. From what I hear, breaking down is quite common. Mark my words, children, a motorcar is for getting around in small areas. I'm going to stick with horses and buggies and the trolley."

"I agree with you, Papa. Them being in danger scares me."

"Not me," said Ben running down the hall. "I'm one fast boy. I can out-run any danger."

"Papa, I learned a new word in school today. Serenity."

The back door slammed shut. Ben was outside running in circles at the wheel of his make-believe motorcar. "Putt, putt, putt, putt, putt!"

Papa sighed. "Serenity is an excellent word, Ociee, but mighty hard to come by with your brother around."

I didn't mention "irksome" to Papa.

*

Ben came home from Ma Gram's with chocolate cookies along with a note saying he was strong in arithmetic. As soon as he read it, Papa called Ben inside.

"I'm mighty pleased with Ethelene's praise. Maybe one of these days you and I'll become a couple of businessmen. What will it be, cotton, lumber, or mules?"

"Right now, I believe I'll have another cookie."

"You have plenty of time, son, all the time in the world."

"Yoo hoo! Anybody home?"

"Mae, Mae's here!" Ben and I rushed to greet her. To our delight, she was carrying a basket.

"I'll be glad when next week comes and Fred will finally get back home," she said. "My husband has been away too frequently for this wife."

Papa kissed her forehead. "I'm to blame. He took off so much time moving us."

"Papa Nash, I didn't mean to complain."

"Of course not, Mae. I didn't take it that way, but I'll always appreciate what he and YOU have done for us."

"Our pleasure, Papa Nash. Is everything going well with you all?"

I spoke up eagerly. "Mae, I'll start. I absolutely love St. Agnes."

Ben put his fists on his hips and said, "My friend Billy Boy's grandmother is my teacher. She makes school fun, well mostly. Ma Gram told Papa I'm a numbers genius."

"How marvelous! I'm pleased you like her," said Mae. "Fred and I met the first tutor. What WAS her name?"

No one could remember the lady's real name. We laughed again.

"I nicknamed her Miss Dreadful . . . " Mae began.

Again, Ben and I giggled.

"Miss Dreadful had marvelous credentials. Fred thought she'd work out well, but I knew better. The unpleasant soul reminded me of a crotchety lady who once taught me. I'll never forget her name, Miss Creel. I must confess, when her back was turned, we horrid children referred to her as 'Miss Cruel.'"

Papa tried hard not to laugh.

"I apologize, shouldn't be such a bad influence on you children. I know Papa Nash expects you to respect your teachers, and well you should."

"It's quite all right, Mae. Truth is, most students will experience a 'Miss Cruel.'"

I looked up at him. "Did you, Papa?"

"Every student, BUT me."

We had a fun-filled visit with Mae. Never one to talk about himself, Papa even mentioned his bookkeeping position. He turned red in the face when Mae praised him.

She also encouraged us about school.

"Fred will be pleased about St. Agnes and Ma Gram."

"Only Agnes is a saint," I said, "Ma Gram is still on earth."

"Huh?" said Ben. Noticing Papa and Mae's laughter, my bother added quickly, "Oh, I get it."

Mae was from the same "cut of cloth" as our papa. Aunt Mamie described certain people that way. Like Papa, our sister-in-law wasn't very comfortable talking about herself. She mentioned Fred's friend, Jason Caldwell.

"Jason says the four of you remain quite a topic in Holly Springs. Dorothy Cardwell goes on and on about 'those charming children, Ociee and Ben.' Annie Kate Milam continues to tell anyone who'll listen about the adventure surrounding the Madstone and her Memphis-bound relatives from Abbeville."

I looked at Papa. "Papa, do you reckon Grannie Dot and Miz Annie Kate will come visit us one of these days?"

"Ociee girl, fine with me, but let's get Mamie here first."

"MAMIE! Mae, you won't believe this," I said. "Aunt Mamie got married and she's bringing her husband to visit!"

"Married? I assumed Mamie would always remain a single lady."

"As did I," Papa nodded, "but my sister up and married George Lynch. Ociee did the matchmaking."

"Did you, Ociee?"

"When you agreed to marry Fred, I started working on Aunt Mamie, but she didn't do one thing about it until Old Horse died. I figured she married Mr. Lynch to help him get over losing his horse."

Papa all but fell off his chair. "Ociee Nash, don't you dare suggest such Aunt Mamie or to George Lynch." He slapped his knee. "My sister! Can't you see a fine woman like her pulling a buggy down Charlotte Street?"

Mae's hat fell off, landing on the floor. "Giddy up, Mamie!" She used her hankie to dab off her giggling tears.

Ben picked up Mae's hat, put it on his head, and began trotting around.

"Y'all, quit!" I squealed.

Then I lost control of my own tickle box and laughed harder than everyone else. I couldn't erase my mind's picture of Aunt Mamie and the buggy going up and down the streets of Asheville.

"I didn't mean my *aunt* . . . "

I was laughing too much to get out my words.

One minute Papa was acting like Ben saying silly things. Next thing we knew, he turned back into being our papa. Clearing his throat he said, "Listen everyone, I have to make one thing clear. This remains our secret joke, Ociee, Ben, Mae and me. My sister would not appreciate our making merry at her expense."

"Well drat," I frowned at Ben. "Even a sweet man like Papa taunts his sister."

Ben made a goofy face, as if he wanted to stick out his tongue but his lips wouldn't let him.

"Listen to me. With all the teasing between a brother

and a sister also comes genuine caring," said Papa. "It's the mark of a close family. No matter what else goes on, we love and support one another."

"What a nice thought, Papa Nash," said Mae, "I never had a sister or a brother, not until I married Fred. Now I have one of each."

I threw my arms around Mae. So did Ben, but he quickly returned to his chair. He didn't want to expose his soft spot. I hugged Mae for much longer. We were a strange bunch of people, us Nashes. One minute we were falling around laughing at a family member. Just as suddenly, we were close to tears hugging Fred's wife.

Mae looked at her pocket watch, "Gracious, look at the time. I'd best be on my way. Please enjoy this basket of goodies. Don't forget to give me more details about Mamie's visit."

Papa nodded. "Ociee tells me she's planning a party for the newlyweds. We couldn't have it without you and Fred."

She smiled. "This 'oldie-wed' will make certain Fred checks his schedule of runs. I'll help every way you want."

I tugged her hand. "I already wrote Aunt Mamie saying you would."

"And well you should, Ociee, because we're sisters," she added, "growing closer each day. I'm delighted you moved to Memphis."

Ben was already into the basket of food. Papa and I walked Mae to her buggy. Papa said, "Too bad we can't hitch up Aunt Mamie."

"Papa, remember it's our secret."

"Oops, I almost forgot."

We all laughed again.

*

I had schoolwork to do, but I couldn't concentrate. *Concentrate*, another new word. I jotted the three words in my journal: *Concentrate, serenity, irksome.*

I asked permission to take a short ride on Maud.

"Be back before suppertime," said Papa.

"I will."

I knew Mae put goodies a-plenty our basket, so I sneaked a cloth napkin from the drawer and tied fudge and two apples in it. No time to write a proper note, I placed my surprise on fever lady's porch.

For you, from O.N.

Chapter 20

For a while, we had no excitement. Papa thought it was a pleasant change. So did I. Ben did not.

As much as I didn't want to stir up trouble, I'd been praying, as Sister Cecilia recommended. I sincerely believed I was being guided to console fever lady. Perhaps the inspiration came to me from Mama.

> *Here is some hard candy for you. If you are feeling sad, sometimes eating a sweet will cheer you. I hope the candy does not hurt your teeth. I brush mine when I think about it. I pray for you. O.N.*

Ben kept his promise and was doing acceptable schoolwork for Ma Gram. According to Ma Gram and much to Papa's surprise, he and Billy Boy were still being good as gold.

In a letter, Mr. Fitch agreed to sell our papa his wagon along with Mule. Papa traded both for a buggy. Because Ben and I weren't attached to the horse, not like we were to Maud, we weren't upset. Actually, we were upset. He and I really wanted a motorcar. We brought up the topic again as we rode to Papa's business.

"Over my dead body," said Papa.

We hushed.

Our papa was pleased with his job at the mercantile store. Now settled, he had decided to take Ben and me over to introduce us to his co-workers. I reckoned it was to show us off. We got to go in our own brand new buggy.

"Look at Maud," I said changing the subject. "Reckon

she likes pulling our buggy better than she did the wagon?"

"She's most partial to carrying you, Ociee."

I got nervous thinking Papa might ask where I'd been riding so much lately. Just then, a large black dog ran in front of our buggy. "Whoa!" It was all Papa could do to keep from hitting the pup as it ran unawares, chasing a squirrel.

Before we knew it, we arrived at the store. Ben and I were so busy behaving, we hardly remembered meeting people. They all seemed nice enough. The main thing was we made Papa proud. In fact, he rewarded us with our second trolley ride. We rode all the way down Madison Avenue. That pleasant springtime afternoon in 1900, Ben and I were in Heaven.

Heaven. I'd just written about it in my journal. To get inside the gates of Heaven Sister says we must try to be good. Mama is waiting for me so I must make it. Because of Sister Cecilia, Sister Gertrude, and Sister Mary Louis, I am not worried. At first, I was concerned about Ben getting to Heaven too. Not now. Ma Gram carries as much influence as the nuns.

It was after dark when we got home. Ben took Maud out back to cool her down and feed her. Papa and I were heading inside to get supper on when we spotted a telegram under the front door. It was the longest telegram I'd ever seen. Papa said it must have cost George Lynch an entire day's earnings.

Will arrive late Friday STOP
Fred arranged rail travel STOP
Family dinner sounds splendid STOP
We love you STOP
Mamie and George STOP

"Papa, can you believe it? They're really coming!" I

danced around the porch, into the yard, and back up on to the porch. I couldn't wait to get my arms around Aunt Mamie and feel her arms around me. "Papa, may we call Mr. Lynch 'Uncle George'?"

"I can't see why not, but you might want to call him 'Uncle Lynch.' It could get complicated to have two fellows named George in the same house."

I ran out back and told Ben.

His face fell. "Ociee, are these people gonna like me?"

Ben's shyness didn't appear very often, but tonight it came rushing to cover him over like a rain cloud. As a rule, Ben was the most outgoing person in our family, friendlier than Fred or Papa, or me. But news of meeting Uncle Lynch and seeing Aunt Mamie for the first time since Mama's funeral washed away his gusto. All of a sudden, my brother became a bashful boy.

"Ben, 'these people' are your family. Like you? They'll love you! And you'll enjoy Aunt Mamie and her husband. Don't you remember the things I've told you about them?"

Papa overheard our conversation. "Ben, fact is, Aunt Mamie already loves you."

"How could she, Papa? She only knows Ociee."

"You are my son, part of me. Why, she'd care about you for that alone. But she'll like you as will George Lynch because of the charming boy you are. Wait and see, you'll have a fine time when they come."

Ben wasn't convinced. I could tell because he was quiet as night.

Papa had an idea. "What do you think about taking them to see the Mississippi River?"

Ben perked up.

"For a picnic, Papa?" I said. "A picnic can be our family party, not just some plain old dinner to celebrate their wedding. We can eat our meal beside the mighty Mississippi."

"*Mighty Mississippi,*" said Papa. "That's one *mighty* fine idea."

Completely missing our papa's joke, Ben asked, "Will we have Fred and Mae with us?"

"Sure we will," echoed Papa and me.

I added, "And we'll pack lunches with lots of sweets."

"Sweets? Your best idea so far," said Ben.

Papa put his hand on my brother's shoulder. "Perhaps we'll even go aboard a riverboat."

Ben all but flew over the moon. "How soon are they coming?"

"Friday, Ben, they're coming Friday."

"Shucks, I have to wait THAT long?"

Ben's bashfulness evaporated like water on a hot roof.

The next morning, I spotted something in the corner of the porch behind the swing. It was a small piece of white cloth. I leaned over and picked it up. Tied tightly in a knot was the napkin I'd dropped off on fever lady's porch. Inside I found a handful of buttons, numerous black and white ones, some purple, some red, along with many tiny pearls.

> *To O.N. I watched your buggy go by last night. I followed. Two decades have passed by since I have been on your street. Do not fear me, for I mean no harm. S.*

How I wanted to tell somebody about fever lady and those buttons! But Ben would get all worked up and blab to everyone. He'd probably beat down her door and demand buttons of his own. Papa would worry himself sick, while Sister Cecilia would be disappointed because I hadn't followed her advice to stay clear of fever lady. I didn't have the faintest idea what to do next. I fretted the whole day. After school, I walked down to Ma Gram's and told her the whole story.

"First things first, young lady. You must talk with your papa."

I groaned.

"You'll tell him tonight, but first you and I have something to do. Ociee, your fever lady says she means no harm. As much as I want to believe her, I'm not convinced. We'll take a buggy ride to pay her a visit."

"Fever lady won't like that!"

"She'll not know."

I hurried home for Mae's basket. Thank glory Papa was at the mercantile store and Ben and Billy Boy were out playing a ball game with neighbor boys. Ma Gram and I filled the basket with goodies and fruit.

> *To S. Your buttons were a dear surprise. Thank you. I will make them into a picture or a necklace. Here is a gift for you. I hope to become your friend. O.N.*

Ma Gram drove me to the end of fever lady's street. She stopped her horse and buggy behind tall bushes so's not to be seen. I jumped down and placed the basket on the porch. I took my time leaving. Even then, S. did not appear.

As soon as Papa got home, Ma Gram arranged for Ben to play checkers with Billy Boy. The house quiet, I stood at Papa's desk. I'd never done anything quite as difficult. Clutching the napkin with fever lady's buttons, I began, "I have something to tell you. I've been leaving cookies and fruit on fever lady's porch."

Papa put down his pen and gazed at me. Disappointment flooded his face.

"I haven't seen her in person, Papa, not one single time." I swallowed. "But last night, she left these for me." I opened the napkin. He read her note.

"Ociee."

"I had to bring her some cheer!"

Papa sighed.

"Today when I talked to Ma Gram, she insisted I be honest with you. We filled Mae's basket and went over there together. Like always, fever lady hid inside."

"I'm pleased you told me the truth, Ociee. It's never good to keep secrets from me, but, dear child, you put yourself in harm's way by making such a serious decision for yourself."

"I know, but, Papa . . . "

"'But, Papa, nothing, Ociee! You are much too young to take on such a task. This is one time your heart grew too big for its britches. I recognize your concern for this poor woman, but you shouldn't have disobeyed me."

I sat there listening

He relented. "At least you used better judgment to confide in Ma Gram."

I let out a gigantic puff of air as worry and guilt evaporated. "I'm glad you know, Papa." I hugged his neck.

"You can tell me anything. I want to think about what we'll do next, Ociee. Do you hear me? I'm saying what WE will do next."

"Papa, your 'we' makes me feel much better."

I felt like I'd crawled out of a deep hole. The air was fresh and my conscience was clear.

As it turned out, the decision was made not by us, but by fever lady herself. On Friday morning, Mae's basket reappeared filled with colored ribbons. They smelled musty, like Papa's fiddle case.

> *To O.N. This is my spring farewell. I go into myself for summer because I die a second time. I die first in November with my beloved in the war during 1863. I*

> *awaken in spring only to die again with my daughter. She passed away with yellow fever in June, 1878. Please, O.N., you must honor my grief until I arise. S.*

"Papa!"

He read her note. "Seems fever lady sets her own rules. Poor woman, I've never read anything as pitiful. A sad creature she is."

"What should we do?"

"Just as she asks."

I decided to take the note to school that morning. I'd keep it in my pocket to show to Sister.

"What's the odd smell?" said Ben, rubbing a night's sleep from his eyes.

"Ribbons from the fever lady."

"What! The witch woman's been here! Did you see her? Did she try to get ME? Bet those ribbons are poisoned!"

Papa said, "Ben, this is a long story. You and Ociee have school, I have work. And Mamie and George are arriving tonight. Go get dressed."

"You can't *do* THIS to me!"

"Sure I can, I'm your papa. Maybe Ociee will tell you during breakfast."

Ben dressed like he'd been fired from a cannon, and he ate even faster.

"Oh, it's nothing really, Ben. I simply looked for goodness instead of any badness. She's sad both inside and out; that's the reason she appears as she does."

"Like a witch!"

"No, Ben, like a woman in mourning. She grieves for her husband and her child. One was killed in the War, the other by yellow fever."

"This is awful, Ociee." Ben was about to cry.

"I know."

I told him as much as time allowed, finally showing him her note. "So we'll have to leave her alone. Papa said so. Do you promise?"

"I promise. I wish she *was* a witch. I'd rather be scared than sad."

Papa shook his head. "Enough of this sorrowful talk, children. It's off to Ma Gram's with you, young man, and off to St. Agnes with you, sweet girl."

Ben raced out the door to tell Billy Boy the news. Papa called me over. "You've had a whole lot of excitement this morning. Think you can calm down enough for school?"

"Sure can, Papa. Fact is, I have something planned."

"Should I be concerned?"

"No sir, I'll tell you all about it tonight."

Papa left for work, and I walked down Orleans. Wearing my locket, I carried my books, the basket, and fever lady's buttons and ribbons, along with Mama's picture.

*

"Sister Cecilia, on Fridays you invite us to share art or songs, sometimes a picture or a story. Today I have something."

"Splendid. Who would like for Ociee to share?"

"We would!"

Giving Sister fever lady's letter, I stood in front of my class. Words flowed from me as peacefully as a spring shower.

"When I was nine years old, I learned a lesson about accepting folks, *even* when they are very different from me and from anyone I'd ever known. One day, my brother Ben and I discovered a Gypsy camped near our old farm down in Mississippi."

The whole class mouthed in awe, "A *Gypsy*."

I told them how our older brother tried to scare Ben and me by saying Gypsies were known for their evil deeds. "Fred warned us saying, 'Best stay away from them or they're gonna GET YOU!'"

My classmates jumped just like Ben and I had. Their eyes still wild, I showed Mama's picture and explained the Gypsy painted it for me after he returned my lost locket and saw her solemn portrait in our parlor. Most importantly, I made them see why Fred had been wrong. Everyone said Mama was beautiful in the Gypsy's picture. And it lifted my spirit for the whole class to realize I really did have a mama, even though she lived in Heaven.

For the second part of my story, I picked up the basket.

"See these ribbons and buttons?"

The girls nodded.

"Got these from a witch woman right here in Memphis."

Mabel shouted out, "A real witch, Ociee, in MEMPHIS?"

Betty leapt from her seat, "And you didn't tell ME?"

"Shhh, students," said Sister Cecilia. Calm yourselves. Sit quietly this instant!"

"Truth is, she's not a witch after all. It's just like the Gypsy man. Both times I thought these people must be bad because they looked odd, looked scary. Like Fred, I was wrong. Inside, the Gypsy was as good as my papa, and the fever lady may turn out to be as kind as Sister Cecilia. If I ever really get acquainted with her."

The girls sat with their mouths ajar.

Sister smiled.

"In last week's list of words, we had *prudence*. Lately, I've worried myself into a tizzy about a bunch of things. To end my talk, I'm going to use our new word in a sentence."

The girls leaned forward in their seats.

"I would have felt a whole lot better about all these adventures if I had used more *prudence*."

"Nicely done, Ociee," said Sister.

Hands flew into the air. Nearly every girl had a question. Sister allowed me to tell a bit more about my Gypsy, but as soon as I finished she cautioned us about putting ourselves into dangerous situations, mostly regarding strangers. I tried not to make eye contact while she was warning us, because I'd not heeded her advice.

Betty wanted to know where the witch woman lived.

Sister Cecilia turned to me. I couldn't help but look back at her.

"She'll be away for the summer."

Sister cleared her throat. "I see."

"Fact is, Sister, she may be gone for good."

Sister let me get away with a little white fib and never said another word about it. After she read fever lady's letter, she understood. Sister Cecilia employed her own holy version of prudence.

Chapter 21

Fred's horse and buggy was hitched in front of our house. I saw it the minute I turned the corner. I broke into a run. I figured he and Mae must have come by to help us get ready for our visitors. My stomach spun around and turned upside down. I'd soon be greeting Aunt Mamie and Uncle Lynch.

"Fred?"

I put my books, Mama's picture, and the basket of ribbons on the table by the front door.

"Mae?"

"Ben, are you home?"

Nothing. He must have been with Billy Boy and Ma Gram.

I peeked in the kitchen, in Papa's room, and in Ben's. Our papa was still at work, but I couldn't imagine where everyone else was, Mae and Fred, particularly. Where would they go without their buggy?

I went in my room to change out of my uniform.

"Surprise!" Aunt Mamie and Mr. Lynch stood up from the other side of my bed. "We got here early!"

I had the same thunderstruck expression as Betty's when I told our class about the fever lady.

Aunt Mamie held wide her arms. I ran to her, bursting into tears. "I missed you so much!"

"I'm here and ever so delighted to see you, my darling girl. Did you notice? Our train arrived early, as did yours when you came to Asheville."

Ben crawled out from under my bed. "Mr. Lynch said Fred telegraphed the engineer and told him the Lynches were in a big hurry, so the train from Asheville traveled twice as fast."

"It worked!" said Mr. Lynch. He pulled Ben to his feet.

Stepping into Mr. Lynch's warm embrace, I said, "I missed you."

"Missed you, too, Miss Ociee. By the way, your brother tells me I have a new name, '*Uncle* Lynch.' It suits me, don't you think?"

"Yes, Uncle Lynch, it does." I squeezed his hand. "I'm so very sorry about Old Horse."

"I know you are, Ociee girl. You always had a carrot for the feller."

"I'm still grieving him. Because I wasn't there when he died, I keep tricking myself into thinking he didn't."

"I'm afraid it's true. We've lost our Old Horse. I loved the grand beast nearly as much as any human I've known."

At first, I thought he might weep, but a man like Mr. Lynch would never let himself go.

Aunt Mamie took Mr. Lynch's hand.

He smiled. "Yep, Mamie and I had a first-rate ride on the train. Didn't have the first minute of trouble. Thanks to Fred, we were treated like royalty."

"Speaking of Fred, he and Mae should be here shortly. They're having a visit with Ben's teacher."

Hearing those words, Ben blushed and turned everyone's attention from his schoolwork to his current favorite topic. "Ociee, Uncle Lynch says he is gonna bring his motorcar next time."

"You *are*?" I recalled my horrifying image of their motorcar tumbling down the side of a North Carolina mountain.

"We'll have to think long and hard about that. Coming by rail is most pleasant," said Aunt Mamie. "Which reminds me, I have an idea, but it'll have to wait for George's approval."

"Which George?" I asked.

"Your PAPA George, that's who."

"What IS your idea?" pleaded Ben.

"Hush up, Ben, you heard Aunt Mamie. She said wait."

"Aw, shucks."

"I'm sorry, Aunt Mamie, Ben can be impatient."

Ben gave me a mean look.

"Ben, impatience runs in the Nash family. It's a mark of intelligence."

My brother loved Aunt Mamie from then on.

"I like to think I'm introducing patience into this family," said Mr. Lynch. As an example, I was extremely patient waiting for your beloved aunt to say 'I do'!"

Aunt Mamie turned beet red. What was it about grown folks getting married that colored their faces? I noticed it first with Mae and Fred, then Aunt Mamie. I wondered if I'd eventually suffer from the blushing nuisance.

"Are you folks trying to have a party without us?" said Fred. He came in with his arm around Mae.

"You two are missing the fun," said Mr. Lynch. "We surprised Ociee but good."

"Good for you. Mae and I've had an interesting visit ourselves."

Ben blushed, but it had nothing to do with marrying. I could tell he was wondering if Ma Gram confided something bad about him.

"Let's have a seat. Ociee and Ben, would you please pour lemonade for everyone? I noticed Papa left a pitcher full in the ice box."

Ben whispered something in Fred's ear.

Fred chuckled. "You have nothing to fear, little man. Ma Gram says you are most energetic."

"Aunt Mamie," said Ben, grinning from ear to ear, "did y'all hear him?"

"Yes, I'm not surprised."

"Nor are we," Fred noted. "Please, Ben, you and Ociee get the drinks. Mamie and George must be parched, and so are we."

"We'll do it, Fred, but don't be telling anything important. We don't want to miss out."

Ben helped me reach Mama's best glasses. We chipped some ice and poured the lemonade. I arranged the drinks on a tray and carefully carried it to the parlor. As we served the drinks, Fred looked my way. "So Ociee galloped off on Maud and brought back the Milam Madstone."

I arched my back and stood all the straighter.

"Ociee wouldn't have had the chance to become a hero if it weren't for me," insisted Ben. "I was the one who got Fred snake bit."

Mr. Lynch choked. "Ben, you certainly have a unique way of explaining things!"

Fred spoke up. "Moving to a big town hasn't deterred these two, not one smidgen. Ben and Ociee managed to find themselves a neighborhood witch."

Aunt Mamie put her hand to her chest. "A witch? I thought Gypsies were your *forte*, dearest."

Ben said, "Is a *forta* anything like a fort?"

Our aunt replied, "No dear. We'll discuss forts at another time. *Forte* means a strong point, one's gift. For example, I would suggest your forte might be your striking enthusiasm."

"My striking enthusiasm, how about that, everybody?"

If my brother hadn't already fallen under Mamie's spell, those words of praise won him over. I knew she could do it.

Mamie continued, "But what's this about a witch?"

"The Gypsy and the witch, actually, they're the same in some ways." I tilted my head back looking up at the ceiling. "Neither one of them had a friend until I came along."

"Ociee, don't you be forgetting," Ben huffed. "At first, they BOTH scared us silly. Why, I had to fight off the Gypsy AND the witch!"

"Hello everyone."

"Papa!"

"George!"

Mr. Lynch replied, "Yes, dear?"

Hurrying to embrace our papa, Aunt Mamie looked back over her shoulder saying, "You know good and well I'm referring to the first George in my life."

"The first? What does this make me, Mamie?"

"George the Second."

Ben said, "Isn't he a king?"

"I AM, Ben," joked Mr. Lynch. "How would you like for me to declare you a royal knight?"

"A royal knight? Terrific, Uncle Lynch."

"Two peas in a pod," said Aunt Mamie.

As I watched our papa exchange hugs and kisses with our aunt, I thought about Ben and me. Would we always be friends? I couldn't imagine us any other way.

"Sorry to interrupt," said Ma Gram. She walked in with Billy Boy. "I happen to have a pound cake. Mmm, it's still warm. Anyone care for a piece?"

"Nashes never turn down cake," said Papa.

He introduced the Williams and asked them to stay for a while. "Sure is nice of you, Ethelene. Let's all gather in the kitchen. Boys, please get extra chairs from the dining room."

I got plates from the shelf above the wood stove.

"Sorry they don't match. We've broken a few. How many do we need? Let's see, Papa, Aunt Mamie, Uncle Lynch, Mae, Fred, Ma Gram, Billy Boy, Ben and me. Ben, you'll have yours on a napkin."

"All right by me. I'm not eating for long. Dessert goes down real fast."

I looked from Papa to Mamie to Uncle Lynch, to Ma Gram and Billy Boy, to Ben, Mae and Fred. We were all together in one spot just as I'd dreamed. It was fitting for Ma Gram to bring dessert. She and Billy Boy had become our "dessert" on East Pontotoc.

*

Later, during supper, Aunt Mamie remarked, "I thought we'd never arrive. As fast as the train traveled, I wished I could blink my eyes and, like magic, be across Tennessee in Memphis."

"If you want to know the facts, your enthused aunt all but drove the train herself," teased Mr. Lynch.

"Reminds me of another Nash girl, a Miss Ociee Nash," said Fred.

"As long as we're talking about trains," said our aunt, "here's a question for George."

Aunt Mamie meant our papa.

"I've heard summers in Memphis can be beastly hot, dear brother, and you're going to be very busy with your job. We'd very much like to have the children come for a visit before school starts. What do you think?"

"I'm gonna ride on a real train!" Ben spit a mouthful of corn all over Mr. Lynch.

Papa arched a brow. "Sister dear, are you sure you know what you're getting into?"

"George, I grew up with *you*, didn't I?"

"Please, Papa, pleeeaase!"

"Seriously, George, our old house needs the sounds of children. Besides, I've all but promised Elizabeth Murphy."

"Maybe I could do without Ociee and Ben for a couple of weeks."

"Hoorah!"

"For now, let's enjoy *this* visit. Now let's clean up these dishes."

I beamed at him. "Yes, sir! Anything you say, Papa."

*

That night I helped Aunt Mamie put her things in my dresser drawers.

"Are you certain you don't mind giving up your room, precious girl?"

"Aunt Mamie, you *need* to sleep in flowers so you won't be homesick. Besides, you'll have my room for only a few days, I have it all the time. Does Uncle Lynch like flowers?"

"Ask him, I don't know. I hope he does. The man is surrounded!"

"Aunt Mamie, I'm glad you got married."

She began to unpack Mr. Lynch's things. Admiring his shirt, my aunt smiled and replied, "As am I." She added, "Ociee, dearest, I know you wanted us to have a lovely wedding similar to Mae and Fred's."

"I understand. Papa said you're a proper lady, and only young folks have fancy ceremonies."

I had enough *prudence* to avoid using the word 'old' again.

"Your letter of congratulations is absolutely dear. Look here, I brought it along."

Toting letters around. "Sounds like something I'd do, Aunt Mamie."

"Well, isn't that natural? We are the Nash ladies, Mae, too."

"Aunt Mamie, we'll pretend you, Mae, and I are 'Ladies in Waiting.' Ben can be the 'Silver Knight,' and Papa, 'King George' with Uncle Lynch, 'George the Second.'"

"Sounds delightful. I love you, Lady Nash."

"I love you, too, Lady Mamie. I can't wait to bring Ben to 66 Charlotte Street."

"Nor can I. Uncle Lynch will have a chum, and I will have my darling girl!"

She hugged me and I hugged her back. The world kept changing, and there were always new adventures around the corner, some sad, some scary, but mostly happy.

So far, so good.

A burst of lavender bathed my room. I knew it was meant for me alone. *Mama, we're going to be okay,* I told her.

I could almost see her smiling.

Acknowledgments

I truly enjoy thanking people. Was raised to be grateful. It's Southern and it's nice. Even so, after seeing their names repeated in my other books, several of my friends and family members insist 'enough is enough'. I'll bend to their wills and not list, line by line, most of the folks who've cheered on my writing throughout the years.

That said, I must mention Emmett and Loftin Propst, our charming grandsons. These boys, ages 4 and 7, can turn a long, exhausting day of work into a fun filled carnival by racing into our kitchen shouting, "My My, Jamey, we're here!"

I also have to put aside my promise regarding a few grown people. One is Deborah Smith of Belle Books. This amazing author and publisher has worked diligently with me to make "The Further Adventures of Ociee Nash" the book it's become. Thank you, too, to J. Kershaw Cooper, for forging the alliance between me and the ladies of Belle Books. Thank you, always, to Dr. Marc Jolley, of Mercer University Press for believing in Ociee Nash in the first place. Was it 1996? Think so.

I will be forever thankful to Kristen McGary and to Amy McGary for bringing to the big screen the characters of "A Flower Blooms on Charlotte Street" in their very fine film, "The Adventures of Ociee Nash." One question frequently asked of me is, "Do you like what they did with your book?" The answer is a resounding "YES!"

As well, I want to single out a few other fellow artists, Jaclyn Weldon White, Beverly and Tom Key, and Jerry Lee Davis. Jerry Lee, my multi-talented friend, are you still willing to play Ociee?

I have to thank Jane Tonning of St. Agnes Academy in

Memphis, Tennessee. This generous lady gave much time and energy to gather historical information about St. Agnes Academy, the school attended by my grandmother Ociee, my mother Mary Catherine Whitman McGraw and me, along with many of the women in our family.

Jane, I hope you will like the parts about our school and not find them too irreverent!

Jane sent me the history of the first 75 years of our school, a history which was compiled in 1925. That's 1925. As I combed through the material, I came across a message from one of the loyal alums.

A long and beautifully written piece, I'll quote a small portion of what she penned.

The seventy-fifth anniversary of the coming of the Sisters of Saint Dominic to Saint Agnes is a great event in the history of Memphis. It is the oldest school in the city. There will be a message of joy borne to many far from Saint Agnes on this Jubilee Day, moving them to unite in spirit with you in grateful thanksgiving for all Saint Agnes has meant to them. It is not easy within the limit of a few lines to do justice to the things that impressed me during the years it was my happy privilege to be a student at Saint Agnes. Many names and events are indelibly recorded in my memory. I was always happy at Saint Agnes and loved each and every Sister under whose instruction I was placed. I have sweet recollections of . . .

One more of my instructors stands out in my memory . . . the one to whom we went with our little troubles and sorrows, the one for whom I still have the deepest love and reverence, Sister Cecilia.

The lovely letter continues on and is signed,

Mrs. Charles Whitman (Ociee Nash)

Finding this message was the highlight of writing my

book. Thank you, Jane.

Our family is in our third century of carrying proudly the Ociee name. Yes, indeed, Ociee Nash Whitman, the heroine of this series, was born November 8, 1889 in Mississippi. Her niece, Ociee Annette Nash Robnett, arrived on July 21, 1914 in Memphis and lives in Houston, Texas, near her son Fred and his family. Ociee's great granddaughter, Ociee Rae Ilg, was born on October 4, 2007 in Colorado and lives with her parents in New Hampshire. My beloved cousin Ociee, now 95-years-old, proudly refers to her great granddaughter as "Ociee III."

It is to the Ociees, all three, I dedicate this book.

Milam McGraw Propst

Follow Ociee's Adventures From The Beginning!

A Flower Blooms On Charlotte Street

Available in ebook from Bell Bridge Books
At Fictionwise.com and Amazon.com

Now that her beloved mother has died, nine-year-old Ociee Nash is the only girl in the Nash family. Even in the modern times of 1900 it's hard to get good grades, learn good manners, and stay out of trouble on her papa's Mississippi farm. Ociee is always up for adventures with her adoring brothers. Deciding his daring daughter needs a woman's influence, Papa Nash sends Ociee to live with her lovable Aunt Mamie in the big city of Asheville, North Carolina. There Ociee makes some fascinating friends, including one of the Wright brothers, but doesn't give up her adventurous ways.

Trade Paperback available from Mercer University Press, 1400 Coleman Avenue, Macon, Georgia 31207

Excerpt

I slipped the dress over my head, brushed my hair and put on Mama's locket. A tag on my dress told who I was and where I was going. Papa had written it out last night. It read:

> *"Miss Ociee Nash, age 9 years, daughter of George Nash from Abbeville, Mississippi, going to Miss Mamie Nash, 66 Charlotte Street, Asheville, North Carolina.*

Papa told me I would have to wear it for the entire trip. I looked in the mirror. "You can do it, Ociee Nash, you can do this all by yourself."

After breakfast we left dishes soaking in the pan of heated water. Fred carried my trunk out to the wagon. Papa had already hitched up Maude to the wagon. He called us to get a move on.

I hurried through our house one more time so I could remember how it all looked. I needed to see it in my memory if I were to get lonesome at Aunt Mamie's. Then I said good-bye to home, placed my new hat on my head, went outside and climbed aboard the wagon.

Ben was fussing more than usual. "Here I am wearing my Sunday clothes, and it isn't even Sunday," he sulked.

"Ben, you're just fuming because I'm going on the train without you."

"That's not true," he fired back. "Fact is, school starts next week. That's all. I don't care about any old train and not about missing you either."

We drove down the dirt road to Abbeville. It looked like it might rain later in the day. Papa didn't even think to play his harmonica.

We rode real quiet for a long spell. I kept looking hard at everything as we passed by the neighbors' farms, houses, and fields. I wanted to remember every tree, every barn, every cow.

Ociee On Her Own

Available in ebook from Bell Bridge Books
At Fictionwise.com and Amazon.

Ten year old Ociee Nash is back for more adventures, trouble and laughter in the sequel to Milam McGraw Propst's award-winning young adult novel, A FLOWER BLOOMS ON CHARLOTTE STREET. Growing up in turn-of-the-century America, Ociee returns home to her family's Mississippi farm after her exciting time living with Aunt Mamie in the big city of Asheville, North Carolina. But things have changed.

Trade Paperback available from Mercer University Press, 1400 Coleman Avenue, Macon, Georgia 31207

Excerpt

Mama died in the measles epidemic when I was eight years old. A year later, I left our farm in Mississippi and came to live with my aunt. Papa believed his sister Mamie could teach me how to be more ladylike. I was more prone to jumping on moving trains and chasing gypsies. Besides, Papa hadn't been schooled in feminine things. He said in a letter to his sister,

> *Mamie, dear, I suppose you would be a better teacher for my Ociee girl than is your rugged old brother. I will have to ponder this for a while, however.*
> *Yours truly, George Nash.*

Although Papa claimed that he wanted me to go, when I got ready to leave, he was sick at heart. He, my brothers Ben and Fred, and I near about fell to pieces at the depot when we said goodbye.

As miserable as I was about leaving my family and mighty scared, too, it was even worse once I got to Aunt Mamie's. I missed my family something awful. Our farm in Marshall County might as well have been way across the Atlantic Ocean, it seemed so far away to me. And being away from them made missing Mama all the worse.

Even so, things had worked out pretty well in some ways. I was "a charming young lady," folks said. I liked Asheville and Aunt Mamie. I liked Elizabeth, too. Papa and the boys had done all right, too, or so they tried to convince me.

LaVergne, TN USA
05 October 2009
159856LV00002B/5/P

9 780984 125807